The Sheeple

GUS FLORY

THE SHEEPLE

ISBN-10: 1544878443

ISBN-13: 978-1544878447

First Published, 2017
gusflory@yahoo.com

THE SHEEPLE

For the truth seekers.

King of the Hill

Bucky was smarter than your average sheep. Stronger, and more handsome, too.

In the vigor and vitality of his youth, he stood atop the hill with head held high looking down at his half-brother Billy.

Billy lowered his head and scratched the muddy ground with his front hoof. He took two steps back and charged forward at Bucky.

Bucky raised up on his hind legs, turned his head to the side, and sprang forward. The two young sheep collided headfirst with a clunk.

Billy staggered backward. His legs wobbled. Then his knees buckled. Billy dropped face first into the mud.

Bucky walked around his fallen rival.

"Are you OK, Billy?"

Billy attempted to stand on his wobbly legs.

"I'm fine."

The young sheep shook his head and tried to regain focus in his glazed eyes.

"Looks like I win again," Bucky said.

"You had the high ground."

Bucky stood on the crest of the hill with bright eyes shining, a smile on his face.

Billy turned and walked away down the hill toward the flock. "I'll get you next time," he muttered over his shoulder.

"Next time," Bucky called out.

Bucky watched his friend slowly make his way down through the high grass to the flock below.

Bucky and Billy were born in the spring and grew up together. Billy, Bucky and the other young sheep of their generation had spent the spring, summer and fall playing together on the hillsides and in the fields, climbing any boulder, log or pile of dirt, charging playfully at each other, butting heads in the friendly, good-natured contests of a sheep's youth. The young lambs nursed with their mothers and were weaned in the summer. They were growing quickly to adulthood. Bucky was growing quickest of all.

In their contests, Bucky had never been defeated. Billy was his only serious rival. Billy butted heads harder than the other young sheep and put a little more effort into the game than the rest of them. But he never could get the best of Bucky.

Bucky inhaled deeply the clear morning air which was fresh and cool in his nose after three days of heavy rain. The view from here atop the hill was spectacular, especially on a day like today. The sky was a clear and brilliant blue. Puffy white clouds sailed above the countryside in the radiant sunshine.

Every year by late spring, the rains would stop and the sun would blaze down, drying the hills, transforming the grass from green to brown. By August, the grass became flammable tinder. A single spark could set the hills aflame. Acres and acres burned every summer filling the sky with plumes of soot and smoke.

The previous summer had been especially hot and dry. But fall had come suddenly and the rains swept in from the Pacific, drenching the parched hills and filling the creek beds with rushing torrents. One storm rolled in after the next, saturating the dry earth with life-giving water that transformed the hills and arroyos from a dusty brown to a lush and grassy green.

Oaks grew in intermittent groves on the slopes of the hills and along the creek beds. The trees were leafless this late in the year. Their thick trunks branched upward into spindly limbs that reached for the sun with thousands of splaying, fingerlike branches.

These rolling hills, fields and valleys were part of a sprawling military training post. The sheep had been brought here as part of the garrison commander's weed abatement program. The commander had drawn up a contract with a local rancher that allowed him to graze his sheep on the post's hills. The sheep reduced the fire hazard by eating away the grass while the rancher got the use of prime grazing land. Bucky had no way of knowing any of this. All he knew was that these hills were home—the only home he had ever known. He loved every hill and every acre. There was nowhere else he would rather be than right here atop this hill looking out across the world on this beautiful sunny morning.

He looked down from the crest of the hill at the flock below. About three hundred sheep grazed peacefully in a pasture at the bottom of the hill. Bucky watched as Billy reached the bottom of the hill and trotted to the flock. Billy walked between the grazing sheep to his mother who lifted her head from the grass and welcomed him with a kiss from her warm muzzle.

To Bucky, the view today from atop the hill was the most beautiful he'd ever seen; the oaks, the verdant green grass, the white sheep grazing below, the sun shining down on all the world. To the west, the coastal mountains seemed to glow against the blue clarity of the sky. It seemed a scene of heaven.

"It's a beautiful world," Bucky said to himself.

On the opposite hillside, Pedro the shepherd sat in the grass with a .22 rifle across his knees and an open book in his hands. Bucky often studied the shepherd curiously. Old Pedro was different from all the animals. He walked around awkwardly on two legs. Instead of fur or wool, he wore clothing over his naked skin, boots on his feet, and a hat on his head. Why did no other creature look and act like him? The humans seemed a species apart.

Bucky often asked his mother about the shepherd. But Mama always gave the same answer. "The shepherd watches over us. That's all you need to know, sweetie."

Bucky caught sight of Stevie the sheepdog lying in the grass several yards from Pedro. The white and black mutt sniffed the air, searching for some scent that caught his attention. His ears were alert to some rustle in the grass. Stevie was always ready at a moment's notice to race down the hillside and confront any danger that might threaten the flock.

Pedro whistled and Stevie jumped to his feet. The dog trotted up the hill to the shepherd. Old Pedro scratched Stevie behind the ears. The dog wagged its tail and lay down next to Pedro who closed his book and stretched and reclined onto his back in the grass. The old shepherd pulled his hat over his eyes. The dog rested its chin on its master's thigh.

"The shepherd watches over us," Bucky said. "The dog protects us."

Bucky heard a baa-baa-baaing from the flock. He could recognize that baa anywhere. His mother was calling for him. She called him to return to the flock.

"I know. I know," Bucky said. "The flock must stay together."

He hesitated for a moment atop the hill. He enjoyed being up here alone looking down at the world. He liked being able to see the entirety of the flock below him. It calmed him to see them grazing peacefully together. He could see all of them down there—all except one.

He searched the surrounding fields for the one missing sheep until he caught sight of him. The lone sheep was named Greg who stood apart from the rest, grazing alone.

Greg grazed along a barbed wire fence about a hundred yards away from the nearest sheep. Greg was older than Bucky and easily recognizable by his dark wool. He tended to graze away from the flock, slowly drifting farther and farther as the morning turned to afternoon, and by evening he was often nowhere to be seen. Bucky's mother had warned him to stay away from Greg.

As Greg moved down the fence line, Stevie could take it no longer. The dog jumped to its feet and bounded down the hillside. Greg saw the dog coming and made a run for it, but Stevie was too swift. Stevie cut him off and nipped at his rump turning Greg left and right, driving him back to the flock.

"The flock must stay together," Bucky said.

The baa-baaing from his mother now sounded angry.

"The sheep who strays gets eaten," Bucky said to himself.

Bucky leaped forward and ran down the hillside through the wet grass to rejoin the flock. He could hear from the tone of his mother's baas that she was upset with him. He hurried down the hillside hoping his haste would alleviate her anger.

Mama

Bucky reached the bottom of the hill and trotted through the field to the flock. He passed the ewes grazing on the wet grass.

"Sheep who stray get eaten," a ewe said as Bucky trotted past.

"The flock must stay together," another said.

Bucky trotted along not paying them any mind. Mama baa-baaed as he approached.

"You had me worried to death," she said.

"Oh, Mama."

"You know the flock must stay together," she said. "Sheep who stray get eaten."

"I know, Mama. Sheep who stray get eaten."

"Goodness, you're almost as bad as old Greg."

Bucky nuzzled against his mother's warm wool. He pressed himself against her. He felt comfort in her warmth.

"Didn't you hear the coyotes yipping and yapping last night?" she asked. "Those coyotes out there are waiting for one of us to stray from the flock so they can snatch us away and eat us for dinner."

"Oh, Mama. I'm not afraid of any scraggly old coyotes."

"You should be. Last winter they snatched away little Mikey and ripped him limb from limb."

Mama looked up at the hills.

"I'll never forget the awful sound of his bleating as they carried him off. Sheep who stray get eaten. Never forget that, Bucky. The flock must stay together. I couldn't live with myself if something happened to you."

"We were only up on the hill, Mama. The shepherd was watching and Stevie was near."

Mama turned her head and rubbed her warm nose against Bucky's shoulder. "Why must you be such a rambunctious little ram? Just like your Papa."

Her gentle touch warmed him inside. He knew his mother meant well.

Papa was a few yards away munching on the green grass. The big ram lifted his head, still chewing while scanning the flock for his ewes.

The ewes never strayed too far from Papa. In fact, they were drawn to him. All the ewes in the flock were downright smitten by him. They swooned whenever he paid them the slightest attention.

Satisfied that all his ewes were accounted for, Papa returned his attention to vigorously munching the grass.

"I must say," Mama said as she gazed at him. "Your Papa is one handsome ram."

"Gross," Bucky said.

A young male sheep grazed absentmindedly and wandered too close to Papa. Papa raised his head and let out a snort. This startled the sheep who suddenly realized he had stepped too close. The sheep jumped back and then slowly backed away with his head lowered deferentially. Papa raised an eyebrow and grunted before returning to chomping the wet grass.

Bucky studied his father closely, then turned his attention to the other male sheep of the flock. Papa was bigger than the rest of them and definitely leaner and more muscular. The young males seemed pudgy and soft compared to Papa.

There were only a handful of adult rams in the flock. They were deferential to Papa. All the sheep in the flock were. They all followed Papa's lead. If Papa was relaxed, they were relaxed. If he was vigilant, they became vigilant. If Papa ran, they all ran.

"I see a lot of Papa in you," Mama said. "You've got his strength. His animal magnetism."

"Animal magnetism?"

"I see him in you, Bucky."

"I don't think I'm like Papa at all."

"Why do you say that?"

"I've tried talking to Papa but he has nothing to say."

"He's a ram of few words."

Bucky remembered last summer before he had been weaned when he had run up to Papa wanting to ask him a question or two about the dog and the shepherd. Why did the shepherd watch over them? Why did the dog protect them? He had a million questions for his father. Bucky had circled behind the big ram, playfully leaping and kicking his back legs excited to be in his presence. Without looking up from the grass, Papa kicked him with one of his hind legs, striking Bucky in the ribs with a hard hoof. Bucky flew through the air and tumbled over the dirt, unable to breathe. The pain was excruciating. Bucky hobbled away back to his mother. Never again did Bucky wander behind Papa, or attempt to ask him any questions.

"I've always been interested in everything around me—the other sheep, the hills, the trees, and all the world's creatures. I don't think Papa pays attention to any of that."

"You inherited your father's strength and stature. But I'm afraid your curiosity and your questioning nature came from me. The world is a big beautiful place, Bucky, but often it's a confusing place. Sometimes it's best to put our questions aside and accept there are things we aren't meant to understand. It took me some time to figure that out. What I've learned is not to question the sheepisms. If you follow the sheepisms, you'll never go wrong."

"What are sheepisms?"

"Sheepisms are what sheep say."

"But what are sheepisms?"

"Sheepisms are slogans, words to live by, passed down through the flock, one sheep to the next. Sheep who stray get eaten. The flock must stay together. The shepherd watches over us. The dog protects us. Outside the fence is danger. Those are the sheepisms you need to know. That's about all a sheep needs to know. But, Bucky, you should also know this, you will inherit this flock someday just as your father did. You'll be the leader, and a better leader than Papa, I think, because you have his brawn, but brains as well. You must learn to use your brain to keep yourself out of trouble, not get into it. If you follow the sheepisms, you won't go wrong. You'll become the leader of the flock and father many lambs. You'll send all the ewes' hearts aflutter."

"Gross."

"Do you see the way Lulu looks at you? She's enamored of you."

"Lulu?"

"Not just Lulu, but all the young ewes."

"Lulu's enamored of me?"

"Oh, goodness, Bucky. She bats her eyelashes, smiles bashfully and blushes whenever you're near. You'd have to be blind not to see it."

"Lulu, huh?"

"Come here, my handsome little ram."

Mama pressed her warm muzzle against his neck and snuggled against him.

"My handsome little Bucky."

"Do you really think I'll be leader of the flock someday?"

"When you butt heads with the other young sheep, have any of them ever bested you?"

"Never. I win every time."

"When Papa was your age, he didn't win all his fights. Not like you."

"Then how did he become leader of the flock?"

Mama looked over at Papa who grazed nearby. He seemed calm and confident and secure in his position. He was a big, powerful animal.

"When your father was young like you, he was big and strong, but he had many challengers. He could easily overpower them, all except one. There was one young sheep he just couldn't beat and everyone knew Papa was desperate to best him. One hot summer day, Papa announced to the flock that he was going to defeat his rival once and for all. All the sheep in the flock gathered round to watch as the two big rams squared off. All of us saw the fire burning in your father's eyes that day. He pawed at the dirt and snorted and then charged. The two rams crashed together with a mighty crack. Your father hit his foe so hard he nearly killed him. The rival ram fell to the dust, unconscious before he hit the ground. Papa strutted around him like a rooster, and from then on, everyone knew Papa was the dominant sheep in the flock."

"There's only one sheep like that who always challenges me. I guess you could call him my rival."

"Do you think he can beat you, Bucky?"

"Little Billy? No. Not ever."

Mama smiled.

"We sheep are born followers. But you, Bucky, you were born to lead. You know what, my handsome little ram? I think before next winter, you'll be the leader of this flock."

Bucky and Mama grazed together for the rest of the day until the sun sank low on the western horizon. Its glowing rays shot out from behind the clouds that had settled over the coastal mountains. The green hills were illuminated by the soft afternoon glow.

A sharp whistle pierced the air. Stevie barked and ran down the hillside to the flock. All the sheep raised their heads and looked in his direction and baaed.

The Corral

Stevie circled the flock, barking and nipping at the sheep, herding them together. They baaed and some scattered, but Stevie worked the flock expertly.

Pedro stood on the hillside watching. He whistled again.

Papa trotted out in front of the flock and headed up the hillside toward him. The sheep followed while Stevie made sure no stragglers fell behind. Papa led from the front while Stevie herded the flock from behind toward the shepherd.

The air was crisp and the wet grass smelled of cold earth. Bucky trotted alongside his Mama as the flock made its way through the grass up the hillside. The sun was setting behind the mountains to the west. The puffy clouds now glowed in golden light. The sun radiated rays of purple and pink across the atmosphere. Beams of sunlight shone through breaks in the clouds and glowed across the darkening sky.

The sheep trotted along together baaing as they ran up the hill toward the open gate of a large corral under a stand of oak trees. Stevie busily herded the sheep toward the enclosure in the twilight.

Papa rushed through the gate and the flock followed. The big ram ran to a trough filled with alfalfa. He reached the trough first and buried his head in the feed. The other sheep kept their distance, cautiously making their way to the trough. Papa turned and snorted and they backed off.

Outside the gate, Greg darted left and right attempting to avoid entering the pen. Greg was behaving more obstinate and rebellious than usual. He was the last straggler. Stevie nipped at him, corralling him toward the gate. Stevie was too quick for Greg. The dog raced around nipping at the sheep's hind legs, finally forcing him through the gate.

As Greg entered the corral, the shepherd stepped forward and kicked him hard in the shoulder with his muddy boot. Greg slipped in the mud and fell over onto his side. Greg's hooves kicked at the air. He scrambled up from the mud, then darted back for the gate but Pedro slammed it shut. Greg crashed headfirst with a crack into the wooden slats.

"Such a stupid sheeple," Pedro said.

Greg shook his head and blinked his eyes as he regained his senses.

The rest of the sheep were busy in the trough. But Bucky wasn't eating. He had been watching the affair play out between Greg, Stevie and Pedro.

Greg stood by the wooden fence looking through the slats. He looked over his shoulder at

Bucky who was watching him. Greg let out a snort, and turned his head away.

Bucky watched Greg for a moment and finally turned and buried his head in the trough. He stood next to his mother and munched away on the alfalfa. It was more delicious and more filling than the grass on the hills. As he ate, he wondered about Greg, and why Greg never ate from the trough like the rest of them.

Soon Bucky was sated. He stood next to his mother, chewing his cud, feeling her warmth as darkness settled over the hills. The sheep herded together, pressing their bodies up against one another as the chill of night fell over them like a shroud. Puffs of mist shot from their nostrils whenever they snorted or sneezed.

A light fog descended on the hill and over the corral. The air was cold and misty but Bucky was warm inside the flock. He stood close to his warm Mama.

It made sense what they all said. The flock must stay together. Together they were warm. Together they were safe. When they were together like this, a warm feeling of calmness and peace settled over him. It was a good feeling. As he felt it, he knew all was right with the world. His gentle mother loved him. And he loved her. The flock was family. It was good to be loved and to have family.

The sheep began to fall asleep. Their breathing was slow and rhythmic. Bucky's eyes grew heavy as he pressed against his mother's warm wool. As his eyelids closed, he felt secure and safe within the flock. But before sleep took hold, his eyes fell onto

Greg who stood alone alongside the wooden fence, away from the flock.

Bucky watched him standing there by the fence and pondered why Greg chose to remain apart.

Greg stood looking out through the slats into the darkness. His dark wool was wet and caked in mud from his fall. Old Greg looked pathetic standing there, cold and alone.

Greg was different. Mama always said that the sheep who strays gets eaten. Bucky wondered when Greg would finally get eaten. If only he would return to the flock. His survival depended on it. Why couldn't he just fit in?

Bucky liked to stay awake on nights like this, thinking. He thought about Greg and about how sad it must feel to be an outsider—to stand apart in the cold and not together with the flock in warmth and safety. Bucky liked to think and this was a good time for it when most of the sheep were asleep. It was a good time to think about the world; about the shepherd, and the dog, and the hills, the squirrels and the hawks, the deer that silently appeared and disappeared into the brush. And about Greg.

Bucky's consciousness faded to dream.

A vision of a dark mountain in the moonlight appeared in his mind's eye. A mighty ram with giant curling horns stood on the mountaintop silhouetted against a brilliant full moon. The ram was magnificent, with its head held high, horns as thick as oak branches. Its horns attested to its strength, power and formidability.

A blood-chilling howl wailed in the night. In the moonlight, the ram looked left and right and then raised up onto its hind legs as the deathly wail carried through the darkness. Ravenous wolves raced unseen up the mountainside. They panted and snarled as they ran in the night. They closed in on the ram, hungry for blood.

The ram's nostrils flared and its eyes opened wide. It cried out in fear as the wolves raced swiftly toward it.

Bucky awoke with a start from his reverie. The sheep were baaing with alarm. A yip-yip-yapping cackled like witches laughter. The yipping and yapping moved rapidly around them, surrounding them as they stood in the darkness of the enclosure. The excited yips were everywhere.

Bucky was confused. Panic was setting in. The sheep baaed and looked left and right and kicked their hind legs.

"Coyotes!" Mama said. "Stay close, Bucky! They're all around us!"

Predatory

The yipping and yapping terrified them. The coyotes were moving in and around them through the darkness. The cackling came closer and closer through the trees until it seemed as if it were coming through the slats of the fence.

The sheep swiveled their ears and jerked their bodies at each yap. Some trembled and shivered in their fear. Nostrils flared. Eyes were wide and flashed as they looked left and right in the darkness. The yipping and yapping seemed to surround them, but the coyotes were unseen in the night.

Then all was silent. Mist rose from the mud in the darkness.

"Where's the shepherd?"

"Where's Stevie?"

"Don't move."

"We'll all be eaten."

"Stay together," Papa said. "The flock must stay together."

The sheep were skittish, in a state of panic, but there was nowhere to run. Bucky tried to stay close to Mama as the sheep jostled and stamped their feet in alarm.

"Stay close, Bucky."

Bucky pressed his body against his mother's. He had heard much about coyotes but had never seen one. The darkness and the yaps and the panic of the sheep magnified his fear of the unseen predators.

"They're inside the fence!"

Bucky heard angry growls and menacing snarls.

"They're in the pen!"

"Billy! Not my Billy!"

The sheep darted to the left and the right, running into each other and crashing off the wooden slats of the fence. Bucky tried to stay close to his Mama as the sheep jostled them, but they became separated in the commotion.

In the darkness, through the panicking sheep, Bucky saw the dark silhouette of a coyote. It held a sheep by the throat with its jaws. The coyote was lithe and lean with long legs and a long bushy tail. Its sleek predatory form thrashed the fat sheep with rapid jerks of its jaws.

Billy bleated and cried as the coyote thrashed him. The predator pulled him backward with tugs of its head, yanking him toward a crack in the gate.

"Billy!" Bucky yelled.

Bucky scratched the ground with his front hoof, lowered his head and charged across the corral at the coyote. He ran harder and faster than he'd ever run in his life, fueled by fear and a desperate need to save his suffering friend. The sheep darted around him as he charged between them toward the coyote.

Bucky's head crashed into the coyote's ribs. He jerked his head upward at the instant of impact, flipping the startled coyote into the air with a yelp.

The coyote landed on its back and quickly flipped onto its feet. Billy scampered back to his mother, bleating and crying for her.

Bucky turned and faced the coyote. The coyote turned its sleek form. Its long furry tail whipped around as it faced Bucky. Its yellow eyes shone through the darkness.

Its hungry eyes narrowed. The coyote focused on its prey, lowered its head and snarled. The fur on its shoulders bristled.

It leaped forward in a flash and seized Bucky by the throat with its sharp teeth.

Bucky bleated and tried to pull away as the coyote's fangs sank deep into his skin.

Another coyote slipped through the gate and ran at Bucky. It snapped its razor-sharp teeth into Bucky's haunches.

Bucky cried out in pain as the two coyotes sunk in their teeth with their strong jaws. The first coyote whipped its head back and forth, thrashing Bucky to the left and to the right, ripping the skin of his neck.

"Bucky!" Mama screamed. "Oh, no! They've got my Bucky!"

Bucky felt hot blood rise in his throat. His bloody tongue extended through his teeth as he baaed in terror. The first coyote pulled him toward the gate as its companion nipped at Bucky's hide with its sharp teeth.

Just as the coyote reached the gate, a loud stomp shook the earth and splattered mud in the air.

Another quick stomp struck the first coyote, which let out a yelp as it released Bucky from its jaws.

Bucky collapsed on his side in the mud. He looked up to see a black silhouette delivering powerful stomps onto the coyote. Cloven hooves struck down at the coyote with strength and anger.

Through the darkness and mist, Bucky recognized Greg stomping at the coyotes with his front hooves, striking them and sending them darting away around him. The second coyote circled around and sprang toward Greg, sinking its fangs into the big sheep's haunches. Greg kicked and bucked his back legs and snorted in anger.

Barks rang out in the night. Stevie charged through the crack in the gate, growling fiercely as he rushed at the coyotes. The coyotes faced off with the dog who snarled in fury, baring his fangs. Stevie ran at the coyotes, barking and growling.

The two coyotes turned and dashed through the opening in the gate. They ran like jackrabbits through the darkness as Stevie gave chase.

A gunshot cracked in the night.

The sheep baaed loudly in a state of high anxiety. They jostled and kicked and bounced off the slats.

Bucky lay on his side in the mud panting hard through his mouth. He felt hot blood flowing through rips in the skin on his neck, haunches and ribs. His red tongue flopped onto the mud as he panted.

"Oh, my little Bucky," Mama said.

He felt her warm muzzle as she licked his wounds.

The gate swung open. Pedro's boots clomped across the mud. The shepherd scanned the skittish flock with the white beam of his flashlight. The beam fell upon Bucky in the mud. Pedro approached and kneeled down, steadying himself with the butt of his rifle. He shone his light onto Bucky, illuminating red blood on white wool.

Bucky looked up at the human kneeling over him, but the bright white beam from the flashlight burned his eyes.

"Poor sheeple. Poor little sheeple."

He felt the man's hand on his side.

The sharp pain from the coyote bites stung and burned and became unbearable. Bucky breathed rapidly. His heart pounded in his chest. He tried to hold on as he felt himself slipping into oblivion.

Rachel

Warm strokes of a hand against his wool soothed him. He breathed softly as he lay on the straw. He slowly opened his eyes and tried to focus on the form above him. Slowly as he awakened a human face came into focus.

This was the closest he'd ever looked at a human face. This face was much different than the shepherd's. The shepherd's was a grizzled old face with wrinkled skin and hard eyes. This face had the soft delicate features of a little girl. She had long wavy brown hair and warm brown eyes.

"Those awful coyotes must've given you a terrible fright."

Bucky's wool and skin were stained orange where iodine had been applied to his wounds.

The little girl sat in the straw on her knees in her jeans and work shirt. Her leg leaned against Bucky's back as she stroked his side softly.

"You're going to be just fine, little sheepy. Daddy said your tough hide saved you."

The little girl sat next to him for quite some time. Bucky was soothed by her gentle voice and her soft hand on his wool.

They were in the stall of a stable in a large barn filled with bales of hay. An old tractor sat in the center of the floor of the barn. Motorcycles in various states of disrepair were leaned against the wall or propped up on their kickstands. A mare and her foal were in the stable on the opposite side of the barn. The mare whinnied and snorted.

"Rachel," a man's voice called out. "Time for dinner."

"I'll be right there, Daddy."

The little girl ran her hand over Bucky's side.

"You sure are a tough little sheepy."

"Rachel."

"OK, Daddy."

The little girl stood and closed the gate of the stall and ran out of the barn.

Bucky lay still in the straw remembering the attack of the coyotes. He was sore and his throat was dry. He was unsure how long he had been here.

He kicked his legs and sprang onto his feet. He turned his head and examined his wounds. The skin around his throat was red and felt raw and his flanks were covered with frightening gashes. He sniffed at the iodine and tried to lick away the stains.

Back in the corral the coyotes had put the fear of death in him. His wounds throbbed but the pain was mostly gone.

He took a few cautious steps forward and felt pain in his throat and on his haunches. He walked gingerly over to the trough and drank down the cool water. The food trough exuded a rich aroma. It was filled with alfalfa mixed with carrots, rutabagas, turnips and beets. Bucky ate the delicious feed until he felt sated. It was the best he'd ever tasted.

Bucky stood alone in the stall. Two doves cooed to each other above him in the rafters. Chickens clucked and rustled their feathers somewhere outside the wall of the barn.

Bucky desperately missed his Mama and the flock. He didn't know where he was or if he'd ever return to them. When sheep were taken away from the flock, they never returned. Whenever the humans came and loaded the sheep into the trailers, the sheep who remained always said those taken were going to greener pastures. But this wasn't a greener pasture. It was a stall in a barn.

He walked over to the gate and peeked through the slats. The barn door was half open. It was twilight outside the barn. A dirt driveway led away through a vineyard.

As he stood looking out the open barn door, a tomcat sashayed across the barn floor and walked in front of him. It was a striped, orange tabby. The cat stopped and turned and looked through the slats at Bucky.

"Hi, there," the cat said.

"Hello."

"Have you seen any mice here in the barn?"

"No, I haven't."

The cat sashayed past the gate. It stopped and turned its head and looked back at Bucky. It placed one claw over its lips.

"Shhhhh."

The orange cat jumped up onto a hay bale and disappeared.

Bucky spent the night alone in the darkness of his stall. He could hear the mare and her foal across the barn from him but couldn't see them through the slats. The horses didn't reply to his baas.

The crow of a rooster awakened him at dawn. As the sun rose in the misty morning, Bucky heard Rachel singing behind the barn. She fed the chickens that clucked and scratched the dirt on the other side of the barn wall.

"Hello, little sheepy."

Rachel closed the gate to the stall behind her. She carried a pail full of feed and a jar of molasses.

"Oh, my goodness. You were hungry. You're going to need more feed."

She emptied the pail full of carrots, rutabagas and beets into his trough. She kneeled down and opened the jar. She dipped a wooden spoon into the molasses and held it out for him.

"Come here, sheepy."

Bucky smelled the molasses. He approached her and sniffed the spoon. He licked it.

"There you go."

It was the sweetest and most delicious thing he'd ever tasted. His short tail wagged back and forth as he licked the spoon clean. Rachel dipped it back into the jar and let him lick it clean again. He finished nearly all the jar when Rachel's father called for her.

She grabbed the pail and the jar and ran out of the barn.

Bucky remained in the stable for several more days. Humans came in and out of the barn speaking in their strange, sing-song tones. They came for the tractor and for the mare and her foal taking them away for hours on end before returning late in the afternoon or in the evening.

Rachel came to the barn every morning and filled his trough with alfalfa and fresh water. She returned in the afternoon after school and sat with him. She tended to his wounds and stroked his wool and spoke to him with her pleasant voice in her human language he couldn't understand. But he was beginning to pick up a word or two.

One morning, she entered the stall and kneeled beside him. She offered him the spoon covered in molasses and he licked it eagerly.

The orange tabby entered the stall and rubbed its side against Rachel's leg. The cat purred as she pet it.

"Oh, Tiger. I think you love to be pet more than you love eating mice."

Rachel returned her attention to Bucky. She scratched him behind his ears.

"You're getting healthier, little sheepy. It's almost time to go home. I bet you want to go back to your mommy, don't you?"

Tiger

Bucky enjoyed Rachel's presence. Her gentle kindness evoked a warm glow within him whenever she was near. His ears perked up when he heard her nearing the barn. He waited impatiently as she fed the chickens each morning. He pranced about his stall when she swung the gate open, his tail wagging rapidly back and forth.

She filled his food trough, let him lick molasses from the spoon and sat with him, stroking his wool and talking to him in her soothing voice.

The humans were strange creatures. He didn't understand them. They were so different from all the other animals. What made them so different? They walked around on two legs and wore clothing. They were slow and not especially strong compared to other animals, but they seemed to control everything. And they had unlimited amounts of food. The humans were very different; they were creatures apart. And Rachel was special among them. Unlike the men who came in and out of the barn, she was kind and loving and caring. She had cared for him after he'd been attacked by the coyotes. She fed him and was helping him heal. He was becoming very fond of her.

The humans watch over us, he thought.

But as much as he enjoyed Rachel's presence, he wanted to be back with the flock and desperately longed to see his loving Mama again.

With each day that passed, Bucky felt stronger. His injuries were healing quickly and bothered him no more.

One late afternoon after Rachel had left him, he stood staring absently out the slats watching a drizzle of rain fall onto the dirt driveway.

As he stared into the drizzle, he felt as if he were being watched. He looked up over his shoulder and saw the striped orange tabby sitting atop a post looking down at him.

"Hi, Tiger."

The cat purred. "Hello… Sheepy."

"What are you doing up there?"

"I'm looking for mice. I smell them. They've been coming into your stall."

"Are they your friends?"

"My friends? Why, yes. My friends."

"Is that why you're looking for them?"

The cat smiled a knowing grin. "Do you know anything about cats?"

"You're the first cat I've ever met."

"I think you don't know much about anything at all."

"There are no cats where I'm from. But there's a dog. I know a thing or two about dogs."

"Dogs are idiots."

"Dogs protect us."

"Protect you from what?"

"They protect us from coyotes who want to eat us."

"I see. I know the coyotes want to eat you and the dogs chase them away. But do the dogs protect you from the humans who want to eat you?"

"Humans who want to eat me? That doesn't make sense."

Tiger leaped down from the top of the fencepost and walked across the stall. He sniffed the straw under the food trough.

"Mice have been here. Keep your eye out for them."

"I'll tell them you're looking for them."

"No. Don't do that. I want to surprise them."

Tiger slipped under the gate, jumped up onto a hay bale and disappeared.

Bucky stood alone in his stall chewing his cud, staring absently out the barn door into the drizzle.

Protect us from the humans? he thought.

He heard the mare and her foal moving about in their stall across the barn. He wanted to ask them where the humans took them every day. What did they see outside the barn? He baaed to them but they did not answer.

A tiny mouse scurried over the straw in front of the gate.

"Hey, mouse."

The mouse stopped and stood up on its back legs and looked up at Bucky. It was holding the end of a carrot.

"Why, hello, Mr. Sheep."

"You're stealing my food."

"Why, yes. I am. You caught me red-handed. But I think there's enough of it to go around, wouldn't you say?"

"There's plenty. But it's common courtesy to ask before you take something from someone."

The mouse smiled. "Mr. Sheep. May I take this bit of carrot home to feed my babies? They're hungry and cold and this carrot might mean the difference between survival and dying of starvation."

"Well, if you put it that way, I suppose it's OK. You may take the carrot."

"Thank you kind, sir."

The mouse turned to leave with her carrot.

"Hey, mouse. There's a cat who's been looking for you."

The mouse stopped and turned. "I know. That cat is always looking for me. You tell that ugly old cat that you've never seen any mice in this barn, would you?"

In a flash, Tiger leaped off a hay bale and snatched the little mouse with his claws. He sank his sharp teeth into the mouse's back with a crunch. The little mouse kicked and twitched, and went still.

Tiger released his fangs from the dead mouse and looked up at Bucky. He smiled a sly smile and winked.

"What have you done!"

"I caught the mouse."

"But you killed her."

"Yes, I did."

"But why?"

"To eat her, of course."

"But the humans give you all the food you could eat. Why would you do such a thing?"

"I'm a cat. It's my nature."

"You're cruel. You're a cruel and evil cat."

Tiger sniffed the dead mouse that he held under his paws. He looked up at Bucky.

"You don't know much about the ways of the world, do you, sheep?"

"I know the difference between right and wrong. What you've done is wrong."

"Just when you think you know everything, you learn something new. I've learned something new here today."

"What have you learned?"

"I've learned that sheep are really dumb."

Tiger stood, picked up the dead mouse with his teeth, turned and walked away over the straw.

He stopped and looked over his shoulder. He held the mouse in his mouth as he looked back at Bucky.

"Thank you for distracting her," he said from the corner of his mouth. "I may not have caught her without your help."

"You're an awful creature."

Tiger smiled. "Ask yourself this, sheep. What do the humans eat?"

He winked and jumped up on a hay bale and disappeared.

Dinner

The barn doors rolled open. Rachel and her father entered and walked across the straw to the stall. The gate to the stall swung open.

Rachel rushed in and fell to her knees beside Bucky. He didn't prance around the stall like he normally did. He stood still as she stroked his back.

"Hello, little sheepy."

She looked up at her father. "I think he's all better now, Daddy."

The big man took a knee and grabbed Bucky under the mouth with his hard hand. He lifted Bucky's chin and examined his neck. He spun him around and examined his flanks.

"He's almost good as new. You've taken good care of him, Rachel. I'm proud of you. We'll take him back to the flock tomorrow."

"You're going home," Rachel said.

The big man stood and walked out the gate.

"Come on," he said. "You've got homework to finish before dinner."

Rachel ran her hand over Bucky's back. "You sure are a strong little, sheepy. I'm going to miss you. But I bet you'll be happy to be back with your mommy."

She gave him a hug and stood and walked out the gate. Her father shut it behind her.

Bucky hadn't understood their words but somehow knew their intent. He knew this would be his last night in the barn.

He watched them walk out the barn door. He gazed out the slats and out the door and wondered what was out there.

He heard the coo-coo-cooing of the doves above.

Tiger was sitting in the straw on the barn floor looking up into the rafters. The cat looked over his shoulder at Bucky behind the gate.

"Don't even think about eating those doves, you terrible cat."

Tiger stood and walked over to the gate, swishing his tail to the left and to the right. He looked up at Bucky.

"You have no idea, do you?"

"No idea about what?"

"About what they have planned for you."

"What do they have planned for me?"

Tiger smiled a knowing grin. "I heard you're going home in the morning."

"Is that what they said?"

"Rachel took a liking to you, but you must return to the flock. They want you out in the pasture eating so you grow big and fat."

"I can't wait go back. I can't wait to see my friends and my Mama again."

"You must be excited."

"Yes, but I'll miss Rachel."

"Don't worry. You'll be back before long."

"I will? When?"

"When the butcher comes."

"Who's the butcher?"

"He's the one who keeps us fed."

"I can't wait to meet him."

"I can't wait for you to meet him, too."

Tiger licked his chops. He raised an eyebrow.

"Mmm. Mutton."

He looked upward and searched the rafters for the cooing doves. He stood, swished his tail, jumped up on a hay bale and disappeared.

Darkness was falling. Bucky was alone. He peered through the slats out the half-open barn door.

He heard rustling behind him. He looked over his shoulder and saw three tiny mice trying to climb up a metal leg of the food trough. The mice froze when they saw Bucky looking at them.

"Shhh," Bucky said.

He approached the little mice that were now huddled behind the leg of the trough.

"Please, Mr. Sheep. Don't harm us. We're hungry. We're only trying to find something to eat."

The little mice were shivering.

"The cat ate our mother and now we're all alone."

Bucky reached in the trough and grabbed a carrot with his teeth. He dropped it in front of them.

"Thank you," they said.

Bucky leaned down.

"The cat is looking for you. He lurks in the hay bales. I'll baa when he's around. That'll be your signal to hide."

"Thank you, Mr. Sheep."

The three mice scurried away with the carrot.

It was dark inside the barn now. A light drizzle fell outside the barn door. Bucky could smell the rain outside. He pressed his nose through the slats and sniffed. To his surprise, the gate swung open.

Bucky took a few cautious steps out of the stall. He stood in the center of the barn in the darkness staring out the open barn door.

Eventually, he walked slowly to the door and peeked outside.

The gravel driveway sloped down a slight incline and curved upward past a vineyard to a large ranch house on a hill. The house was alight in the darkness, strung with Christmas lights along the eaves and corners. The windows glowed from the warm light within.

On the long sloping lawn in front of the house, a horse, a cow and a sheep looked down at a human baby in a manger. The animals and the baby were bathed in light that contrasted sharply with the surrounding darkness.

Bucky walked out of the barn and down the driveway. He stepped cautiously up the lawn to the animals. None were moving. He nudged the sheep with his nose. But it wasn't real, just a plastic imitation meant to look real.

Bucky looked up at the ranch house outlined in twinkling lights. His curiosity got the best of him. He walked up the lawn to the house. He pushed through a hedge toward a large bay window that glowed from the warm light inside. He raised his head and looked through the glass.

In the living room was a fireplace with a roaring fire. Next to the fire stood a tall Douglas fir tree strung with ornaments and lights.

Rachel lay on her belly on the floor in front of the tree with an open book in front of her. She scribbled in a notebook with a pencil.

"Time for dinner, honey."

Rachel closed the book, stood, and walked to the dinner table where her father sat waiting. Her mother set plates on the table and sat down with them. They bowed their heads in prayer. Then they lifted their forks and knives and cut into their meal.

A large salad bowl centered the table. On their plates were mashed potatoes and asparagus and peas. Bucky sniffed the air and took in the appetizing aroma. But mixed with the aroma was a sickly smell.

He looked closely at their plates. Between the potatoes and vegetables and bread, they were cutting into slabs of something that was definitely not a fruit or vegetable. They cut it with their knives and pierced it with their forks. They put chunks of it into their mouths and chewed and swallowed with great enjoyment.

Bucky sniffed the air and caught the sickly scent between the more palatable aromas. To Bucky, it smelled like death.

His eyes went wide.

It was burnt animal flesh. Meat. They were eating meat.

He felt sick as he watched Rachel put a piece of meat into her mouth and chew.

He stepped back from the window in horror. A wave of disgust washed through him.

Barks rang out. The dogs had caught his scent and were running toward him. They barked and woofed as they sprinted through the darkness.

Bucky ran as fast as he could down the lawn and up the gravel driveway. He scrambled into the barn. He rushed into his stall, grabbed the gate with his teeth and slammed it shut behind him.

Return to the Fold

Rachel and Rancher Dave came into the barn early the next morning. She and her father led Bucky out of the barn to a trailer that was hitched to the back of a red pickup truck. They coaxed Bucky into the trailer and then slammed the gate shut. The engine revved and the truck and trailer lurched forward in a crunch of gravel. They drove past the ranch house, past the vineyards and white wooden fences and the horse pastures beyond.

The horses grazed in the green fields in the morning sunshine.

The truck turned onto a highway and headed north in the cool morning air. A barbed wire fence lined the highway. Beyond the fence, cattle grazed on the hills that were covered by a scattering of leafless oaks.

The truck soon turned off the highway and pulled up to a military gate. Rancher Dave spoke to the soldier at the guard shack. The soldier walked around the truck and looked down at Bucky inside the trailer.

"You're good," the soldier, and waved Rancher Dave forward.

The truck drove onto the military post. They drove past rows of beige two-story barracks lined up row upon row around an airfield, then past warehouses where military vehicles were parked in motor pools.

Rancher Dave turned the truck onto a road that wound between green hills. They drove through the hills for quite some time until turning onto a muddy, dirt road that wound up a steep hill and followed the top of a ridgeline. They bounced along the road under the oaks and splashed through puddles until finally coming to a stop.

Rancher Dave turned off the rattling engine. The truck's doors opened. The gate to the trailer swung open.

"Come on, little sheepy," Rachel said. "You're home."

Rachel and her father coaxed Bucky out of the trailer. Bucky jumped down onto the muddy road and looked around. He recognized this hill. He saw the corral under a stand of oaks. He saw Pedro's truck with a camper on the back parked next to the shepherd shack.

Bucky breathed in the cool morning air and looked out at the green hills that he loved. He caught the scent of sheep.

Pedro and Stevie walked up the hill to them. Stevie ran toward Bucky and quickly got behind him and nipped at his haunches. Bucky kicked his back legs and ran forward. He spotted the flock grazing at the bottom of the hill and bounded down the hill toward them as Stevie barked.

The sheep stopped grazing and looked up. Bucky heard his mother bleat for him. He could recognize that sound anywhere.

He ran down the hill as fast as he could and into the flock as the sheep baaed with excitement. He ran up to his mother and slid to a stop in the wet grass.

"Oh, Bucky. My little Bucky."

He pressed his body against hers. Bucky and his Mama snuggled against each other baaing as the rest of the flock gathered around them.

"Oh, my little Bucky, I love you so."

"I love you, too, Mama."

She took a step back and examined him. Her eyes were full of tears.

"When they took you away, my heart was broken. I thought I'd never see you again."

She cried as she rubbed her muzzle under his chin.

"I can't believe you're home."

The sheep came up to them one by one to examine his wounds and welcome him back to the flock.

"Thank you for saving me from those coyotes," Billy said. "I thought they had me for sure but you came and saved the day. I can't believe you actually head-butted a coyote."

"It was nothing," Bucky said.

Lulu looked at him with wide eyes, examining the red scratches on his haunches and throat.

"You're so brave, Bucky. I'm happy you're OK. I'm so happy to see you."

"I'm happy to see you, too."

The sheep each came to him and paid their respects. Papa stopped grazing only briefly to watch the goings-on, but then returned his attention to munching on the grass.

Soon, the excitement died down and the sheep returned to grazing. Bucky remained by his mother's side. They grazed together in the morning sunshine.

"I thought for sure I'd never see you again. When the humans take sheep away to greener pastures they never bring them back. But here you are back in the fold."

Bucky smiled at her.

"Did they take you to greener pastures, Bucky? Greener than this one?"

"No, Mama. They didn't take me to greener pastures. They took me to a barn."

He told her about the barn and Rachel and the molasses, and about that terrible cat Tiger and the mice.

Bucky looked up at her quizzically. "Mama?" he asked.

"Yes, sweetie?"

"What do humans eat?"

"The humans? Why, human food, of course."

"What kind of food?"

"Humans eat human food."

"Yes, but what kind of food? They don't graze on grass like we do."

"They eat human food. Isn't that enough to know?"

"I saw them eating, Mama."

"Perhaps they eat alfalfa. They always seem to have enough of it for us."

"I saw them eating meat."

Mama looked at him gravely, then looked away.

"Don't be silly."

"But I did, Mama."

Mama nuzzled against her son.

"You're delirious from the excitement of the day."

"I saw them eating meat. They burn it and then cut it with knives and stuff it into their mouths."

Mama stepped away from him. She was obviously upset. "That's crazy talk. The humans watch over us and take care of us."

"I saw it, Mama."

"I don't want you talking like this. Whatever you think you saw, I don't want you to mention it again. Do you understand?"

Bucky saw the anger in her eyes.

"Humans eating meat. It's ridiculous. They watch over us and feed us and protect us from wild animals that really do want to eat us."

"But, Mama—"

She shushed him and turned her back on him. She went back to grazing.

"I'm sorry, Mama."

She paused and turned.

"Please, Bucky. Don't speak like this again."

"OK, Mama."

She smiled and nuzzled against him.

"I'm so happy you're back, sweetie. You acted rashly in the pen when you charged the coyotes. I don't ever want you to risk yourself like that again, do you understand? I know you're a brave little ram but I couldn't stand to lose you again."

She looked over at the sheep in the flock.

"You are such a brave little ram. They all think you're a hero now."

"It's Greg who's the hero. I would've been taken for sure if it wasn't for him."

"Greg?"

"Didn't you see him? The coyotes had me in their jaws but Greg rushed in and stomped them like a bull. He stomped them with his left hoof and with his right. Didn't you see it?"

"I don't think so, sweetie. Greg only thinks of himself."

"No, he scared the coyotes away."

"Oh, Bucky."

"Where is he?"

Mama pointed with her nose across the field. Greg was grazing alone near a grove of oaks far from the flock.

"He saved me, Mama."

"That doesn't sound like something Greg would do. Maybe in the confusion of the moment, that's what you think you saw. Everyone was mad with fear."

"No, Mama. Greg was strong and fearless. A true hero if I've ever seen one."

"Oh, Bucky."

The sun was shining down through the clear blue sky. The hills were lush and green. Bucky couldn't be happier back with the flock. He left his Mama and joined the young sheep.

They played in the grass and talked about the night the coyotes came and how Bucky had charged at them and saved Billy from certain death. Bucky told them how Greg had attacked the coyotes and stomped them with his hooves, but none had seen it happen. In all the confusion and fear and pandemonium, no one had seen what Greg had done.

The young sheep lazed in the sunshine and grazed in the grass with the flock until their bellies were full.

Bucky lifted his head and looked out at the sunlit hills. He saw Greg grazing alone. Bucky looked over his shoulder at Mama who grazed peacefully with her head down in the high grass. He turned and walked across the field toward Greg.

The Black Sheep

Bucky walked through the high grass. Greg grazed along a barbed wire fence. As Bucky got closer, Greg stopped grazing and raised his head and watched as Bucky approached.

"If it isn't the fortunate son."

The old sheep was missing several teeth.

"Hello, Greg."

"What do you want?"

"I want to thank you for what you did in the corral."

Greg looked silently at Bucky for a moment. He chewed his cud.

"Thanks," Bucky said.

"Hmph."

Greg returned his head to the grass and resumed munching.

"It was brave what you did. The coyotes had me. I would've been a goner for sure if you hadn't stomped them like you did. You stomped them with your left and with your right and with your left. It was awesome to see."

Greg continued grazing along the fence without looking up. Bucky watched him for a long moment.

"Why do you stray from the flock, Greg?"

He ignored Bucky's question. He let out a belch.

"Don't you know that sheep who stray get eaten?"

Greg raised his head from the grass. "That's what sheep say."

"No matter what everyone says about you, I'm grateful for what you did. I wish you'd come back to the fold."

"What do they say about me?"

"Nothing."

"Tell me."

"They tell us to stay away from you."

"Is that all?"

"They say you're not a team player. You don't follow the flock. You only care about yourself. They say you're not like the other sheep and that you think strange thoughts."

"They say all that, do they?"

"They say those who stray from the flock get eaten and sooner or later you'll be eaten."

"Yet, here I am. Uneaten."

Greg returned his attention to the grass.

"Don't you know the flock must stay together? Why do you stray from the flock?"

"I have my reasons," he said from the corner of his mouth.

"What are they? What are your reasons?"

"You ask a lot of questions."

"Tell me the reasons."

"Maybe I got tired of listening to sheep say the same things over and over again—repeating the same few thoughts. Maybe I got tired of sheep and their stupid sheepisms."

Bucky stood silently watching Greg graze.

"I have to be honest. I get tired of it, too."

Greg stopped eating and lifted his head. "Do you now?"

"They say the same things over and over. When I ask Mama why things are the way they are and why we think what we do, she can never give me an answer. She just repeats the sheepisms. The flock must stay together. The shepherd watches over us. The dog protects us. Everyone repeats the sheepisms but no one can tell me why the shepherd watches over us, or why the dog protects us."

"We sheep have never been known as deep thinkers."

"I like to think about things but Mama says my curious nature will get me into trouble."

"She's right. It will."

Bucky looked back across the field at the flock. Mama's head was down as she grazed. She hadn't noticed that Bucky had strayed from the flock.

"So, you were with the humans?" Greg asked.

"Yes, they took care of my wounds."

"When sheep are taken away by the humans, they never return. I've wondered where they take us. The sheep say to greener pastures, but they really don't know. No one knows where they take us."

"They didn't take me to greener pastures. They took me to a barn."

Bucky told Greg about his time in the barn—about Rachel and the molasses and the mice.

"Greg, do you know what the humans eat?"

Greg narrowed his eyes. "I have an inkling."

"I saw what they eat."

"Come, walk with me. Tell me."

Greg walked to the barbed wire fence.

"Outside the fence is danger," Bucky said.

"That's what sheep say."

"Stevie will come for us."

"He lets me wander along the fence. He knows I can't get far. It's when I stray away from the fence that he comes for me."

Bucky walked next to Greg. They walked together along the fence through the high grass.

"Before your father was leader of the flock, there was another leader. His name was Zeus. He was bigger than your father and smarter. He was smart for a sheep, perhaps too smart. He was a great storyteller and much loved by us all. One fateful day he called the flock together. We all gathered around him and he told us that he had something serious to tell us. He told us that he had learned a terrible secret, that when the humans come and take sheep from the flock, they don't take us to greener pastures, but to a slaughterhouse where they cut our throats, butcher us, and eat us."

Bucky's eyes went wide.

"Zeus told us that he was organizing our escape. We would escape together and live in the mountains away from the dog and the shepherd. But his speech didn't go over well with the flock. The sheep said the shepherd watches over us and the dog protects us. They couldn't believe that the humans who fed us and kept us safe would betray us. And eat us? They said it was crazy talk. Some said Zeus had lost his mind. Why would the shepherd watch over us and protect us and keep us safe only to eat us? The humans weren't predators like coyotes or cougars. We had an agreement with the humans. We gave them our fleece for their clothing and our milk for their cheese. In turn, they protected us from the wild animals that wanted to eat us. Humans weren't wild animals. What Zeus said didn't make any sense. There was dissension in the flock. If we left the humans, who would protect us? There's danger beyond the fence. We would be eaten before we could make it to the mountains. That night in the corral, Zeus stood up on his hind legs and grabbed the string that opens the latch to the gate. He pulled the string with his teeth and the gate swung open. He called for us to follow. Only the most loyal ewes and rams went with him. I went with him. We ran from the corral but Stevie came after us. In a moment of doubt I hesitated and was chased down by Stevie who brought me back to the flock."

"What happened to him? What happened to Zeus?"

"We never heard from him again, or from any of the sheep who escaped with him. But over the years, rumors spread down to us from the wild animals— the deer, the rabbits and the jays. They say there's a flock of wild sheep that lives free atop Liberty Mountain."

Greg pointed with his nose through the barbed wire fence toward the coastal mountains in the distance. Far away beyond the green hills and valleys and over the oaks was a mountain ridge that held back a fog bank.

"Zeus and his flock are up there on Liberty Mountain."

The fog rolled over the edge of the ridge in wisps. One peak jutted upward through the fog.

"What did you see when you were with the humans?"

"I saw them eating meat."

"Just as I always suspected. Zeus was right. They eat us. But the flock will never believe it."

Bucky's mother called to him from the flock. She baaed with alarm.

"Your Mama's calling."

"We have to tell them, Greg. We have to tell them the humans are going to eat us."

"Bucky, come back," Mama called over the grass. "The flock must stay together."

"You better go."

"Thank you for saving my life, Greg."

Greg looked at him for a moment.

"Hmph."

He returned his attention to the grass.

Bucky trotted across the field back to the flock and to his Mama. When he reached her, he saw the anger and concern in her eyes.

"I told you to stay away from him."

"Oh, Mama."

"You were near the fence. Outside the fence is danger. The flock must stay together. I don't want you talking to that crazy old sheep again. Do you hear me? He'll try to corrupt your mind. He's bad news. Bad news."

The Fence

Bucky grazed under an oak on the side of a steep hill. Mama grazed quietly next to him. The sheep of the flock grazed around them in the tall grass. The flock moved slowly across the hillside under the afternoon sun.

"Did you know Zeus?" Bucky asked.

Mama looked up from the grass.

"Did Greg tell you about Zeus?"

"He told me that Zeus escaped to the mountains after learning that the humans eat meat."

"I warned you about Greg. His mind is twisted. He's spent so much time away from the flock that his thoughts have lost connection with reality."

"Did Zeus run away from the flock because he learned that humans eat meat?"

Mama sighed.

"Zeus was a great leader. We all loved him. But his mind got away from him. Perhaps it was a sickness, some bad mushrooms he ate while grazing, maybe rotten alfalfa. We saw it developing over time. His mind became impaired and his thoughts erratic. He started believing things that weren't true. It's a shame. But it can happen to the best of us, Bucky."

"Maybe he was right, Mama."

Mama looked at him with deadly seriousness.

"Please, Bucky. You have so much life ahead of you. The young rams all look up to you. The ewes are enamored with you. You're next in line to lead the flock. Please don't speak this way. You have so much to lose."

"Greg said Zeus escaped to the mountains and he lives in freedom there now."

"Zeus and the sheep who followed him are all dead. Outside the fence is great danger. Coyotes and mountain lions and all kinds of hungry predators. Zeus and his sheep didn't get far. They were eaten long ago."

"Maybe Greg is right and they live free in the mountains."

"No, Bucky. We're sheep. We're not wild animals. And Greg is a crazy fool. Zeus and his followers are all dead and gone. Now, please, don't speak of this again."

Mama return her attention to the grass. She was obviously tense and upset.

Bucky grazed alongside her in thought. They grazed through the afternoon. As they grazed, Bucky slowly moved away from his mother, allowing the distance between them to grow. When Mama disappeared around the hillside, Bucky turned and walked in the opposite direction to Greg who was grazing at the bottom of the hill away from the flock.

Bucky approached him.

"Didn't your Mama warn you to stay away from me?"

"She did."

Greg shrugged and went back to grazing.

"Mama said Zeus is dead."

"Maybe," Greg said, without raising his head from the grass. "Or maybe not."

"Is there any way to know for sure?"

Greg lifted his head and looked at Bucky.

"Perhaps. Follow me."

He turned and walked to the fence line. Bucky looked back up the hillside at the flock. Half the sheep had disappeared around the other side of the hill. Stevie and the shepherd could not be seen. Bucky turned and followed Greg.

They walked through the tall grass along the barbed wire fence. A light breeze blew over the grass in waves. On the other side of the fence, a deer and her fawn grazed in the chaparral on a hillside.

"The deer might know," Greg said.

Greg and Bucky walked along the fence and looked through the barbed wire at the deer. But the deer were too far from the fence.

"They're beautiful," Bucky said.

"Beautiful and free."

The doe looked at them from the hillside as she chewed her cud. Her big black eyes watched them for a moment.

"Hey, deer," Greg called. "Come here, deer."

The doe turned and disappeared into the chaparral with her fawn.

"I guess they didn't want to talk," Greg said. "Oh, to be a deer. Wild and free."

"They move swiftly with such grace," Bucky said.

Greg resumed walking along the fence. After a time they came upon cattle grazing on the hills on the opposite side of the fence. Cows and calves and large bulls stood in profile on the green grass with their heads down as they grazed. Greg and Bucky walked along the barbed wire until they came upon a giant black bull munching on the grass just beyond the fence line. The bull was massive and muscular with enormous hooves, big black eyes, a huge wet nose and sharp, curved horns.

"Excuse me, Mr. Bull," Greg said.

The bull snorted without looking up from the grass.

"Do you know if there are wild sheep that live in the mountains?"

The bull snorted again. It turned its back and defecated.

"Gross," Bucky said.

"You, sir, are a disgusting animal," Greg said.

The bull kicked the earth with its muscular hind legs, spraying Greg and Bucky with grass and mud and manure.

Bucky and Greg quickly moved back from the fence. They continued walking along the fence line, shaking the mud and manure from their wool and picking off the grass with their teeth.

"He was a rude old bull," Bucky said.

"If only we sheep were that big and strong."

"We wouldn't have to worry about coyotes."

"No, we wouldn't. If I were a bull, I'd stomp those coyotes good."

"I'd gore them with my horns. Then I'd defecate on them."

"Yes, I'd defecate on them, too."

On the other side of the fence, a ground squirrel stood on its hind legs atop a pile of dirt looking up at the sky.

Bucky and Greg stopped and looked up with it.

"What are you looking at?" Bucky asked.

"A red-tailed hawk is on the hunt," the squirrel said. "If you see him, call out, would you? We prey species need to stick together."

"OK," Bucky said.

"Squirrel," Greg said. "Have you heard of a flock of wild sheep that lives in the mountains?"

The squirrel looked at them quizzically and scratched his chin.

"Wild sheep? Now that is a strange concept. With the coyotes about and Puma on the prowl, I don't suppose domesticated sheep like yourselves would last long beyond the fence line. Not without a dog protecting you."

"There was a sheep named Zeus who escaped the flock a few years back," Greg said. "Word has spread through the wild animals that he lives free in the mountains with his flock."

"Come to think of it, a squirrel once told me about a flock of giant sheep that lives near the coastal range. Yes, it was quite a tale. Mighty rams as big as horses with enormous racks of antlers. They rule the countryside. There's a giant herd of them. When they run the earth shakes. Their pounding hooves collapse the burrows and holes of the squirrels who live there."

"Giant sheep?" Greg asked. "Is one named Zeus?"

A hawk let out a screech above them.

"Take cover!" the squirrel exclaimed. It scrambled to its hole and disappeared down it.

The hawk hovered above them in the blue sky, flapping its wings rapidly as it looked down intently for prey.

"Squirrel, come back," Bucky called.

"We've wandered far enough," Greg said. "Stevie's probably noticed we're gone by now. We better get back before he decides to run down here and sink his teeth into my brisket."

Greg turned and walked back along the fence. Bucky followed.

"Sheep as big as horses?" Bucky asked. "With antlers? Do you think that squirrel was pulling your leg?"

"Maybe. Maybe not."

"Maybe they are up there wild and free."

"It's nice to think so."

"Mama told me I shouldn't talk about Zeus because one day I'll be the leader of the flock."

"A leader can frighten the flock with crazy conspiracy theories about humans eating meat."

"I can't get it out of my head. I saw them eating meat. The humans keep us here and protect us so they can eat us."

"You're next in line to lead the flock. The rams and the ewes will follow you. You'll sire many lambs. You'll lead a good life if you can put these thoughts out of your mind."

"Why is everyone so sure I'll lead the flock?"

"You're stronger and faster than the other young sheep. There's a reason for this. Do you know what it is?"

"I was born this way."

"No, that's not it. Do you remember when the lambs were taken away by the humans and their cries carried across the hills?"

"Maybe I do. I was so young then."

"They left you with the flock and you avoided their painful fate. That is why you are stronger."

"What did the humans do to them?"

Greg stopped walking and stood still in the grass.

"Come here. I'll show you."

Gelded

"Come here and look," Greg said.

He lifted one of his hind legs and motioned with his nose for Bucky to take a look.

Bucky examined the skin between Greg's legs.

"What do you see?"

"Something's missing."

Bucky looked between his own legs and then back under Greg's.

"Do you see what's missing?" Greg asked.

"They're missing all right. Where are they?"

Greg lowered his leg and walked slowly along the fence line. Bucky walked beside him.

"In the early summer, the humans come to the flock and gather up the male lambs. They hold us down and cut us with their knives. They castrate us one by one. We scream and cry from the horror and pain they inflict on us. It's a terrible thing. I was a young lamb when they cut me. The others don't remember. They don't want to remember. But I do. I'll never forget that day when they castrated me."

"Why would the humans do such a thing?"

"I'm sure they have their reasons."

"What do they do with them after they cut them off?"

"The shepherd is the one who cut me. He cut them off with his knife and tossed them into a bucket, then moved on to the next lamb. I stood there in the grass in shock looking at that bloody bucket. Stevie ran up, stuck his head in the bucket and ate them."

"He ate them?"

"I will never forget seeing him standing over that bucket looking at me with that bloody grin. All these years later, and I say this with all honesty, that was the single worst moment of my life."

"No kidding."

"When they were finished, they returned us to our mothers. When we returned, I realized there was one lamb who had been left behind who did not suffer the way the rest of us did. That lamb's name was Bonehead. He wasn't the brightest sheep in the flock, but he had been spared the pain the rest of us were forced to endure. Eventually, the pain faded and our wounds healed. Things returned to normal. We lambs played again in the fields and the hills. I was the biggest lamb of my generation. I stood out from the rest because of my size and my dark wool. Like you, I was stronger and faster than my peers. When we butted heads, I always won. No other young ram could defeat me. Bonehead was my most determined challenger, but I always got the better of him. As the months passed, we lambs matured and grew bigger. But Bonehead was different than the rest of us. He was more interested in the ewes and they were more interested in him. We got larger and fatter but he grew leaner and more muscular. My clashes with him became close-fought battles and more fierce. Then, one day, Bonehead loudly issued a challenge for me to face him for a fight. All the sheep in the flock heard his boasts that he was going to defeat me once and for all. They all gathered round as we faced off in the field. I was ready for him, ready to defeat him once more and assert my dominance. He lowered his head and scratched his hooves in the dirt. At that moment, I saw a fire burning in his eyes—a fire that burned more brightly than mine. We charged and our heads collided in a mighty crash. Bonehead hit me with such force that I thought my skull had cracked open and my spine had shattered. I fell unconscious onto the dirt. When I finally came to, I saw Bonehead strutting over me with his nose in the air. All the sheep baaed their approval. I attempted to stand but I was paralyzed. My ears were ringing and my vision was blurry. I was certain I was about to die. It was plain to all and to myself that I was no longer a match for Bonehead. I was defeated. We all knew that he was the stronger ram. I lay there alone in the dirt for hours until finally I recovered enough strength to stand. But I was severely weakened. I could barely see and the ringing in my ears would not stop. It hurt to walk, to eat and to drink. It took me months to recover, and by then Bonehead had grown even larger and stronger. He took leadership of the flock. In my weakened state, I watched Bonehead have his way with the ewes and dominate the rams. I wondered how he had gained the upper hand. What was different about him from the rest of us? What was the secret to his strength and power? Then I remembered, that unlike the rest of us, he hadn't been taken away that day and castrated."

"Bonehead is Papa?"

"Yes. No one calls him Bonehead anymore. They all call him Papa now."

Greg and Bucky walked in silence through the grass.

"I remember that day now when I was a little lamb," Bucky said. "The humans came and took the other lambs away. They left me behind."

"And you're stronger than the rest of them, leaner and more muscular. They can't defeat you, no matter how hard they try."

"Are you saying I have an unfair advantage?"

"The humans didn't castrate you like they did to the other young rams because they want you to be the next leader of the flock. They want you to take possession of the ewes and sire many lambs."

"It's not right. It's not right that they did this to them but not me."

"I've been watching the humans for years now trying to understand their ways. Most sheep are uninterested because their minds are incapable of comprehending the humans, of comprehending most things. Every now and then, the humans come to the flock and take sheep away and we never see them again. We say they take them to greener pastures, so we tell ourselves. They bring new sheep to the flock. Some of us are taken and other others arrive. Where do they take us? Why do they keep us here?"

Greg stopped and looked about. "I think we walked too far. We've been gone a long time. I don't think I've ever been away this long without Stevie coming for me."

"Should we return back?"

"No, we can go up the hill here. The flock should be on the other side."

Greg and Bucky climbed up a small cliff, clinging to the steep dirt face with their hooves. They scrambled over a ledge and into an oak grove on the hillside. Green lichen drooped like Spanish moss from the leafless branches. The grass under the trees was especially lush and green. A light breeze blew down the hillside.

They reached the top of the hill. The corral where they were held at night stood under the oaks a short way down the ridge.

A truck pulling a large trailer bounced away on the road that ran along the ridgeline. They watched the truck drive away into the distance.

"I wonder what that truck was doing here?" Bucky asked.

"Look there," Greg said. "The shepherd shack."

The Shack

A small wooden shack stood at the end of a dirt road. The shack was on the edge of the hilltop looking out over the hills and valleys. Pedro's old pickup truck with a camper atop its bed was parked on the muddy road by the shack.

"That's where the shepherd sleeps," Greg said. "I don't see him. Or Stevie."

"They must be with the flock," Bucky said.

"Stevie must've noticed that we're gone by now. He's probably looking for us. If he catches wind of us up here, he's going to be angry. We should head back to the flock."

Bucky looked at the truck and camper parked in the road on the ridge. He looked at the wooden shack set under the oaks.

"Let's take a closer look," Bucky said. "I want to know what the shepherd does up here."

Greg sniffed the air and looked left and right. His ears swiveled on his head.

"I don't know about this."

The two sheep walked past Pedro's old truck and around the camper. The camper and truck were beat up and dented. A lawn chair was propped against the back of the truck near the camper door. A coffee can filled with cigarette butts was next to the chair.

The two sheep walked away from the truck and up to the wooden shack. It wasn't much to look at, just a small wooden building overlooking a grassy plain and the hills beyond.

At the far end of the plain was a river. The banks of the river were lined with oak trees that grew thick on the water's edge. Way off in the distance, the coastal mountains could be seen against the gray backdrop of the winter sky. The sun was shining through breaks in the clouds but a dark cold front was moving in from the ocean beyond the mountains.

Bucky pushed on the shack's wooden door with his nose. The door swung open. He poked his head through the doorway. No one was inside.

"Come on."

"Maybe we should go," Greg said. "It smells like humans in there. I've never liked their odor."

"It smells like the shepherd."

Blankets and a pillow were atop a cot against the far wall. Books were stacked on the floor against the wall near the cot. Paperbacks, hardbacks, a dictionary, manuals; all kinds of books in stacks that leaned or had collapsed onto the floor. A small portable television sat silently on a nightstand. A space heater was on the floor but emitted no heat. In the center of the room were a table and two chairs. An empty coffee mug and a glass ashtray sat on the table next to a tattered copy of Fyodor Dostoevsky's *Crime and Punishment.* A plastic packet of jerky was next to the thick book. A gas stove was set on a counter next to a window. A silent coffeepot was atop the stove.

Bucky baaed.

He heard no movement inside the shack. He stepped cautiously inside. His hooves clopped on the wooden floor.

"This is not a good idea," Greg said. "If the shepherd catches us, we'll feel the heel of his boot."

"Let's find out what he does in here."

"Bucky."

Bucky walked across the floor and nosed around the cot. The shepherd's scent was heavy on the pillow and blankets—sweat, cigarettes, alcohol, chilies, soap and grease. It was the same scent he sometimes caught on the wind when it blew from the shepherd's direction.

Greg hesitatingly stepped through the doorway.

The pelts of two coyotes were nailed to the wooden wall. Greg examined them.

"This explains why we haven't heard those coyotes yapping at night. The shepherd took care of them. He's been watching over us."

"Look at these blankets," Bucky said, examining them closely.

Greg walked up and sniffed them.

"Wool," Greg said. "They make them from our wool and fleece."

"Is that why they shear us?"

"I would say so."

"Aren't they strange?" Bucky asked. "The humans have no fur or wool of their own, but use ours to keep themselves warm."

"They are strange creatures."

"Look, here's where Stevie eats."

Greg sniffed the empty metal bowl in the corner of the room.

"Does it smell like meat?"

"Maybe. I can't say. It smells disgusting, that's for sure."

Greg spotted an apple on the nightstand. He sniffed the apple and bit into it with a crunch.

An old faded photo on the nightstand depicted the shepherd with a woman and three young children.

Bucky nosed around a wastebasket filled with empty beer cans. His lip curled at the foul smell.

"They are strange," Bucky said. "Why are they so different from all the other animals? I wish I knew their secret."

"They're just smarter than the rest of us. We go along with all the shearing and the castrating and the taking of our lambs because we're too dumb to do anything about it."

"I've been watching the shepherd. He doesn't appear to be much smarter than us. I think his two hands give him an advantage. He can shoot a gun and drive a truck. If sheep had hands like a human, maybe things would be different. We would be their equals."

"Sheep with rifles driving around in trucks?"

Bucky walked across the floor to the table. He sniffed the mug, ashtray and book on the table top.

His nostrils flared and his eyes went wide.

"Greg. Look here."

Greg chomped on the remains of the apple as he clopped over the wooden floor to the table.

They examined the plastic packet on the table. Strips of jerky were inside the clear package.

"It smells like death," Bucky said.

Greg sniffed the package, then turned his head away.

"It's dried animal meat. Probably meat from a sheep. It has the smell of a lamb carcass. I smelled a dead one before when one of our lambs that had gone missing was found after several months dried by the summer sun."

"Is it lamb meat?" Bucky asked.

"I can't say for sure. Hopefully, it wasn't someone we knew."

"The shepherd watches over us. That's what they say. Then he comes up here and eats our friends."

"Whether it's from a lamb or not, it's definitely meat. I knew Zeus was right. The humans are meat eaters. They watch over us and let us graze and get fat and then they take us away to eat us."

"I hate them," Bucky said.

A bark rang out. Bucky and Greg looked at each other with alarm.

"Stevie!"

The two sheep scrambled toward the door, their hooves clattering against the wooden floor. They ran out the doorway away from the shack.

Stevie sprinted up the hill through the grass toward them with blood lust in his eyes.

Stevie

Bucky and Greg raced down the hill as fast as they could. Stevie shot like a dart through the grass and circled around behind them. He sank his teeth hard into Bucky's rump.

Bucky cried out in pain from the bite as he raced toward the flock. He had been nipped by Stevie before, but never this hard.

Stevie ran around and then bit hard at Greg's haunches.

The two sheep ran fast through the grass, but it was futile attempting to escape the dog's sharp teeth.

Stevie barked and nipped at the two sheep, separating them as they neared the flock. Bucky tried to stay close to Greg to no avail. Stevie cut him off and drove him away from his companion, quickly whipping around and driving Greg toward the flock.

Greg sprinted to the flock but Stevie kept turning back and blocking Bucky's way. The swift canine let Greg go and turned his attention solely onto Bucky.

Bucky made a break for the flock but Stevie jumped in front of him and barked. Bucky feinted left and right, trying to get past, but Stevie's nips and barks were relentless.

He realized there was no getting past him. In his frustration, he lowered his head and charged. Stevie jumped out of the way and nipped Bucky on the thigh.

Bucky spun around, lowered his head and charged again. But Stevie easily sidestepped him and nipped him hard again. Bucky gave it a few more goes. Finally, he succumbed to exhaustion. He stood still, panting heavily, looking down at Stevie.

The dog lay motionless in the grass like a Sphinx.

"Your move."

"I want to go back to the flock."

"Back to your Mama?"

"Why won't you let me pass?"

"You and I need to talk."

Bucky cocked his head sideways and studied the dog.

"I don't ever want to see you near the shepherd shack again."

"We didn't mean any harm. We were just looking around."

"Don't go up there again, do you understand?"

"But–"

Stevie growled and showed his sharp teeth.

"Do you understand?"

"Yes."

"And I want you to stay away from Greg. That old sheep is nothing but trouble."

"He's my friend."

"He's a loser."

"But—"

"Stay away from him. Nobody likes a black sheep."

Stevie looked over his shoulder at the flock. He sniffed the air and listened with his pointed ears. He spotted his master sitting on the hillside above the flock. The dog returned his gaze to Bucky.

"Master has big plans for you. Sooner or later, you're going to take over the flock. I want you to watch your father, the way he leads the sheep. Your Papa and I have a good working relationship. I want you and I to have a good working relationship, too."

"Why does everyone keep saying I will take over from Papa? Where's Papa going?"

"Nowhere for now. But he's getting old. The flock will need a new leader. It needs a good leader when your Papa's gone. It needs you. Soon the time will come for you to take over."

"When?"

"Soon enough."

"What if I don't want to be the leader?"

"I've been watching you. You're still young but you're big and strong. The other sheep look up to you. You'll be a great leader if you can get your head in the right place. I know what I'm talking about. I've worked with many rams over the years. Some are better leaders than others. Your father has been a good leader. He's solid and dependable. He doesn't overthink things. But I've noticed the other sheep like you, Bucky, more than they like Papa.

They'll follow you anywhere. With the two of us working together, we can make a great team. We can keep Master happy. What I need you to do in the meantime is keep away from Greg. Don't let him corrupt your mind. Then you and I will get along swell."

"You've worked with many rams?"

"Quite a few now."

"Did you know a ram named Zeus?"

Stevie looked at Bucky curiously, then looked away to the mountains.

"You've been spending too much time with Greg. Much too much time. Yes, I knew Zeus. He was the best leader I've had the privilege of working with—the greatest I've known of your breed. In fact, he and I became close friends. That was my mistake. In our line of work, it's better to keep our relationship on a strictly professional basis. Like the relationship I have with your father. I learned that the hard way."

"What happened to Zeus?"

"I've already said too much. You get back to the flock and remember what I've told you. Keep your head in the game. And stay away from that old black sheep. You hear me?"

Bucky nodded. Stevie stood and moved aside to let him pass. They trotted together through the grass. Stevie broke away and headed up the hill to Pedro as Bucky entered the flock.

He noticed a sadness in the eyes of many of the ewes as he trotted past them. He heard his mother bleating. She was calling for him urgently.

"Oh, thank goodness, Bucky. I thought they had taken you, too."

"Taken me?"

"I've been searching everywhere for you."

Bucky looked around and noticed that many of the young sheep were gone.

"Where's Billy?"

"While you were away, the shepherd, the dog and the rancher came down the hill with several men. They herded us into the pen and separated us. Most of the young sheep were driven into a chute that led into the back of a trailer. Billy, Tom, Ricky, all the young rams from your generation, were loaded on board. Rancher Dave came into the flock and examined the rest of us. He clipped my ear."

Bucky examined the yellow tag clipped onto his mother's ear.

"What could it be?" Bucky asked.

"Rancher Dave and the other humans got into the truck and drove away with the young sheep. They took them to greener pastures. But I'm not ready for them to take you."

"I think they took them away to eat them."

"Bucky. Don't speak like that. The humans are strange in their ways but they're not predators. Every now and then they come and take some us to greener pastures. That's the way it's always been."

"Has anyone ever seen the greener pastures?"

"Of course. Plenty of sheep have seen them."

"Who?"

Mama thought it over. "Well, no one who's seen them has returned to the flock. But if they had, they would tell us all about them."

"I've seen things, Mama. I've seen what they eat."

"Bucky. I've told you once and I'm telling you again. Don't speak this way. Especially in front of the ewes whose lambs have been taken. You'll only hurt them more."

"Lulu," Bucky said. "Did they take Lulu?"

"No, she's still here."

Bucky was relieved to hear that Lulu hadn't been taken, but he worried about Billy and his friends.

He walked away from Mama and searched the flock for the young sheep he'd grown up with. All the young males were gone.

Bucky spotted Lulu grazing by her mother. He ran to her.

"Oh, Bucky. I'm so happy to see you're still here. I thought they had taken you to greener pastures."

Bucky walked up to her and nuzzled her with his muzzle. It was the first physical affection he'd ever shown to a ewe.

She was taken aback, but then pressed her warm nose against his.

"Oh, Bucky."

Suddenly, the emotions overwhelmed him.

"Poor Billy," he said. "Poor Billy."

Lulu

Lulu recounted how the humans had herded them into the pen and separated the young males from the flock. The ewes cried out as their sons were driven into the chute. The males cried for their mothers when the truck pulled away.

"It was frightening," Lulu said. "But my mama says this happens every year. They take some of us away. Sometimes they bring new sheep to the flock. Don't be upset, Bucky. It's just the way of things."

"Where does your mama say they take them?"

"My mama says it's to a better place—where the grass is green all year round and the sky is always blue, and there are no coyotes or eagles that snatch away little lambs."

"I've seen things, Lulu," Bucky said. "I've seen what the humans eat."

"What the humans eat? Everyone knows what the human eat."

"What do they eat?"

"Why, human food, of course, you silly."

"Yes, but what is human food?"

"It's what humans eat."

Bucky was growing frustrated with her. "Yes, but what kind of food? What do they actually eat?"

Lulu looked at him quizzically. "Well, I'm not sure. I've never really thought much about it."

"I've seen what they eat. They eat meat."

"Meat? Like coyotes?"

"I think they took our friends away to eat them."

Lulu laughed. "Now you're really being silly. Humans eating meat like coyotes."

"I've seen it, Lulu."

She giggled. "Oh, Bucky. You're teasing. We all know the shepherd watches over us. He doesn't eat us. The humans protect us from predators who want to eat us. If it weren't for the humans, we'd all be eaten for sure."

"Listen to me, Lulu. I think they keep us here, keep us safe, so they can eat us."

"You're serious."

"After I was attacked by the coyotes, they took me to a barn. I snuck out one night and looked into a human house and I saw them eating. They were eating meat."

"Bucky, you were sick. You probably thought you saw them eating meat, but it was something else. After all, they took care of you after the coyotes tried to eat you. They wouldn't do that if they were meat eaters, too."

"I know what I saw, Lulu."

Lulu saw that Bucky was upset. She stepped up to him and ran her muzzle over his cheek.

"I know what I saw. Please believe me."

"It's just too hard to imagine. Humans eating meat. I don't see how it could be possible. The shepherd would have to be in on it, and Stevie, and Rancher Dave. And Papa, is he in on it, too? It would be quite a conspiracy. It doesn't make any sense, Bucky."

"I know it doesn't. But I know what I saw."

"So you think they took Billy and Tom and Ricky and all the young sheep away to eat them? Do you know how crazy that sounds?"

"I know it sounds crazy, and for their sake I hope it's not true. But the shepherd eats meat. He has meat on his table in the shepherd shack."

"The shepherd? But he's watching us now." She looked up at the shepherd sitting on the hillside. "Why doesn't he try to eat us if he's a meat eater?"

"I don't know, Lulu. Maybe he's not hungry now."

"Oh, Bucky."

"You don't believe me, do you?"

"Bucky, think rationally for a second. Can you imagine the humans eating our friends? It's too terrible to contemplate, if it weren't so ridiculous. It would be an awful thing knowing that all of us are kept here on the hills and in the fields just so they could eat us. No one could believe that."

"Greg believes it."

"That explains it. You've been talking to Greg."

"Yes, I have. He's wiser than you might think."

"Greg believes there's a kingdom of wild sheep who live beyond the fence up in the mountains."

"How do you know it's not true?"

She laughed. "Wild sheep? Beyond the fence? Everyone knows there's danger beyond the fence."

"I'll show you what they eat, Lulu. I can prove it to you. Come with me to the shepherd shack."

"Oh, Bucky. Can we talk about something else?"

Bucky was angry. She had a look in her eyes as if he were being foolish and she knew better.

She ran her muzzle over his neck but he stepped away. He didn't want to talk to her anymore. He walked away from her. He walked through the flock and kept walking until he was away from them all.

He stood alone and grazed in the high grass keeping his distance from the flock. The thought of his friends being eaten pained him. The fact that Lulu didn't believe him angered him. But as much as he was angry at Lulu, he hoped he was wrong and she was right that the humans had taken their friends to greener pastures.

But he couldn't shake the thought of what he had seen. It was vivid in his mind. He saw Rachel, her father and mother cutting and stabbing dead animal flesh and shoveling it into their mouths. He remembered the smell. The memory nauseated him.

The sun was low on the mountains. Its winter rays illuminated the western sky in pastels of pink, yellow and red. The countryside was alight with a fading afternoon glow. The hills and the trees cast long shadows across the grass. A chill was in the air.

The shepherd whistled. Stevie ran down the hillside barking.

Papa trotted up the hill and the sheep followed him as Stevie rounded up the stragglers. Greg trotted away and Stevie bolted after him, quickly catching him and herding him back to the flock.

Bucky walked slowly up the hillside behind the flock. Stevie ran up alongside him.

"Let's move, Bucky. You're dragging. You should be up front with your Papa. Lead from the front."

Stevie bounded away after an older ewe, nipping at her, urging her to keep up.

Papa ran through the gate into the pen and buried his head in the trough. The flock followed him in.

Bucky stood outside the gate as the stragglers rushed in around him. Greg was the last to rush past him. Bucky stood in front of the gate not entering.

"I'm not liking what I'm seeing, Bucky," Stevie said. "Don't disappoint me. Don't disappoint all of us."

"I know why you keep us here."

Mama bleated for him from within the pen. She sounded worried and alarmed. Lulu watched him with worry in her gentle eyes.

"We keep you here for your protection," Stevie said as he circled around Bucky.

"No, you don't. I know why and I'm going to do something about it."

"Get a grip on yourself," Stevie growled.

Stevie nipped Bucky hard on the haunches. Bucky kicked his hind legs and sprang forward into the corral.

Conspiracy Theorist

Darkness fell over the hills. A full moon shone brightly in the night sky.

Bucky sulked as he stood within the flock. The sheep pressed themselves against each other in the confined space of the pen. Some were already sleeping, breathing heavily and methodically. Bucky stood quietly next to his mother who pressed herself against him. But he stepped away from her.

The bright white disk of the moon shot silver beams through the fingerlike branches of the oaks that swayed in the winter night breeze. Bucky saw Greg standing alone in the dark against the wooden fence.

Bucky pushed his way through the flock to him.

"Come to join the old black sheep, have you?"

"I feel like we have to do something. I can't just go back to life as normal after knowing what I know."

"You're upset because they took your friends. But they didn't take you. That's something to be grateful for."

"They didn't take me, but sooner or later they will."

"Perhaps. But for now, they've got other plans for you."

"I can't stand the thought of it. I can't stand the thought of all of us living here in ignorance believing things that aren't true."

"It is what it is."

"I can't stand the thought of the humans killing my friends. Eating them. And all of us here just go on with our lives as if everything is normal. It's not right. They need to know the truth."

"What if they did know? What good would it do? Maybe it would make matters worse."

"No. It's better to know the truth than to live a lie. If they knew the truth, we could do something about it."

"Do what?"

"We could escape this place. Like Zeus did."

"For all we know, Zeus has been dead for years."

"We need to get out of this place."

"You're being rash, Bucky. Think things through."

"I'm going to tell them, Greg."

"I don't think that's a good idea."

Bucky walked away from Greg and stood at the edge of the flock.

"Everyone," he said. "I have something to say."

The sheep were pressed together, many half-asleep. The silver moonlight shone down on them through the tree branches. The branches danced above them in the wind.

"Everyone. Can I have your attention? I have something important to say."

The sheep began to stir.

"Bucky has an announcement to make."

"Bucky?"

"Our little Bucky?"

"At this hour?"

"It must be important."

"What on earth could it be?"

"Listen up," Bucky announced. "I have something important to tell all of you. It's something I've learned that we all need to know."

All their eyes were upon him. They watched him quietly in the moonlight.

"It's often said that the shepherd watches over us. That the dog protects us. But no one asks why. Why do they watch over us and protect us? The night the coyotes attacked, I was badly injured and the humans took me away. They took me to the ranch and nursed me back to health in the barn. The night before I returned to you, I snuck out and walked up the hill to the ranch house. I looked in the window and saw the humans eating. I saw them eating meat."

"Did he say meat?"

"I think he said beets."

"They were eating dead animal flesh. Meat."

"Like the coyotes do?"

"Today, Greg and I were at the shepherd shack. We went inside and looked on the shepherd's table. There was meat on the table."

All the sheep were watching him, quietly now.

"Greg put him up to this."

"I'm going to tell you why the shepherd watches over us and why the dog protects us. They watch us and protect us and keep us here and keep the coyotes away so that they can someday take us away and eat us. The humans are meat eaters."

The sheep stood unmoving, staring at him. Their eyes reflected the silver moonlight.

"I know it's a horrible thing to contemplate. I didn't want to believe it myself, but I know what I saw. The humans come to the flock and they take some of us away. We never see them again. We want to believe they take us to greener pastures. To a better place. But I'm afraid that's not the case. They take us away to kill us and cook us and eat us."

"What an awful thing to say."

"Please listen to me. Some day they will come for me, for you, for all of us. They will bring us here to the corral, separate us from the flock, drive us through the chute and into the trailer and take us away. But it doesn't have to be this way. We can escape this place. We can make our way across the fields and through the hills to the mountains, away from the humans where we'll be safe. We can go there and find Zeus and his flock of wild sheep. We're going to get out of here, because, I for one, do not want to be eaten, and I don't want that for any of you. Follow me and we can all be free."

Bucky turned and walked up to the gate. He lifted himself up on his hind legs and pulled himself upright against the slats balancing himself against the fence with his front hooves. He craned his neck and reached for the latch at the top of the gate. He stretched his body and extended his lips. But for all his effort, he couldn't reach the latch. He struggled and hopped on his hind legs and pawed at the slats, straining his neck for the latch. His hooves clattered against the wood. He struggled harder, jumping and extending his lips. He was coming to the unfortunate realization that he wasn't tall enough to reach the latch.

He looked over his shoulder. All the sheep were watching him, unmoving, their eyes aglow in the moonlight.

He turned back around to the fence and continued his struggle, becoming more and more desperate as it became clear that the latch was out of reach.

Greg walked up to him and stood behind him. The old sheep kneeled down and lowered his neck.

"Step on my back."

Bucky lifted up a back hoof and stepped onto Greg's neck. He pawed at the slats with this front hooves, clattering as he lifted himself up to the top of the gate. He extended his lips at the rusted metal latch. But there was no string to pull on. He bit at the latch with his teeth, trying to pull on it, but there was no way to open it. He wrapped his lips around it and bit at the metal. He struggled desperately, his teeth scraping and chomping at the hard, rusty metal.

He lost his balance and slipped off Greg's back, falling hard onto his back with a whump. The hard fall knocked the wind out of him. He lay stunned in the mud for a moment. When he regained his senses he kicked his legs in the air and rolled over onto his stomach.

He shook his head, still not seeing straight from the force of the fall.

He looked up and saw all the sheep of the flock looking down at him, their eyes reflecting the moon. They stared at him silently.

Bucky didn't know what to say. He sensed their disapproval.

Papa pushed his way through the flock and walked up to him. Bucky lay in the mud looking up at the big ram. Papa looked down at him imperiously.

The big ram lifted a hoof and then stomped it hard onto Bucky's head. The blow was so powerful that it stunned Bucky, nearly knocking him unconscious. Papa stomped him again and then again. His hooves rained down onto Bucky's head, neck and back. With each forceful blow, Bucky felt his bones would crack. He struggled to get up on his feet but this only made Papa stomp harder.

Bucky collapsed limp onto his side on the cold ground. Papa stomped him a few more times for good measure.

Bucky lay motionless. His mouth was open, his face pressed against the earth. His bloody tongue was limp in the mud as he panted in the cold air.

The moon shone down through the swaying tree branches. Papa looked down on him in disgust with eyes alight from the moon. Papa turned and walked back into the flock.

"Bucky," Mama said. "My poor little Bucky."

Bucky lay motionless on the wet ground as Mama ran her warm muzzle over his bloodied face.

Outcasts

A bright sunrise illuminated the land. Frost covered the grass, refracting the morning sunlight in tiny pinpoints of light. Mist rose off the frost. The mist rose from the shadows of the gullies and hillsides like steam into the brilliant sunshine.

The shepherd opened the pen and led the sheep down the hill. He led them past the field and the hills they had been grazing for the past few days. The once tall and unruly grass was now cropped short, giving the landscape a tidy appearance. The shepherd led them into an arroyo. Papa followed the shepherd while Stevie made sure the stragglers stayed with the flock. They entered a narrow path between chalky cliffs. Atop the cliffs, the trunks of gnarled oaks reached up between piles of boulders. Lichen drooped from the leafless branches.

Bucky walked alongside his mother. Each step brought aches and pain. His head still throbbed from the thrashing the night before.

Bucky walked with his head down. The other sheep looked at him with sidelong glances before looking away.

"What were you thinking?" Mama asked. "They all think you're crazy."

"I'm not crazy."

"Why would you do such a thing?"

"I know what I saw."

"You don't know what you saw. I don't want you to mention it again. Do you understand? I want you to keep quiet for a while. Just keep quiet and behave and maybe the sheep will forget."

"I don't want them to forget."

"Bucky, please. You can't expect to lead the flock if you act like this."

"Maybe I don't want to lead a bunch of stupid sheep."

"Bucky, don't speak like this. You've angered your father. I tried to calm him but he said he would sooner kill you then let you lead the flock. It's going to take some doing and some time, but you have to win back his favor. You have to win back all their favor. Papa is getting older now. His teeth won't hold out much longer. And his knees. We need you to lead us."

"Lead us to the slaughter?"

Mama looked at him angrily.

"That's enough."

She sped up and walked in front of him pushing through the sheep on the path.

The flock funneled through the narrow arroyo. They stepped over large stones and made their way around boulders and through chaparral in the tight confines between the two cliffs. Mama disappeared in front of him as the sheep jostled through the narrows.

In his pain and soreness he had trouble keeping up.

"Let's go, Bucky," Stevie said. "You're dragging again."

Stevie looked Bucky over and noticed that something was wrong.

"Looks like you lost a fight. And there's only one sheep in the flock strong enough to beat you. What did you do to make Papa mad?"

Bucky trotted along silently. He had no desire to talk to Stevie.

"I'm worried about you, Bucky. Your head is not right. I want you to start looking on the bright side of things again. Get your old exuberant self back. It's a beautiful morning. We're going to a new hill where the grass is fresh and green. Now cheer up and get up there with the flock."

"Can I ask you a question?"

"Sure. Go ahead."

"Papa and Greg have been with the flock a long time now. I understand why Papa is here. But why Greg? Why hasn't he been taken away like the other castrated rams?"

"Ha ha. You're a curious one, aren't you? I wish Greg had been taken away years ago. Believe me. But, you see, all this flock belongs to Rancher Dave, all except Greg. Rancher Dave gave Greg to Master as a token of his appreciation. Master has been keeping Greg here all these years waiting for the day when his family comes to visit from his country. But they haven't come."

"And what happens when his family comes to visit?"

"They will have a great feast. And Greg will be the guest of honor."

"As the main course, you mean."

"You are a curious one. Too curious for a sheep. I want you to keep your head in the here and now, do you hear me?"

"Can I ask you another question?"

"No more questions."

"What do you eat, Stevie? What kind of food?"

Stevie jumped back and nipped Bucky on the haunches. He nipped him again causing Bucky to run forward to the flock.

Stevie darted back and chased the last sheep through the arroyo. The flock emerged onto a frosty field that was quickly thawing in the morning sunshine. They followed the shepherd up a hillside covered with a tangled mass of overgrown grass. The grass was fresh and green and reached above the shepherd's waist. The old shepherd sat on a rock, lit a cigarette and pulled a paperback book out of his jacket pocket. The flock began to graze in the sunny spots where the frost had melted.

Bucky spotted Greg and walked over to him.

"That was quite a speech last night," Greg said. "Riveting. But you need to work on your closing."

"You told me there was a string on the latch."

"I told you Zeus pulled a string on the latch. But that happened many years ago."

"I never would've tried to open the gate if I knew the string wasn't there."

"I tried to warn you."

"I thought if they knew the truth they would follow me."

"You didn't think things all the way through. For someone so smart, you don't know the first thing about sheep, do you?"

Greg looked at Bucky, smiled a gap-toothed smile and laughed.

"You should have seen yourself jumping for that latch with all of them watching. They didn't know what to make of it."

"Thank you for helping me, Greg. No one else would."

Greg shook his head still smiling. "You're one crazy sheep," he said.

"That's what they all think now."

Bucky stayed with Greg. They grazed apart from the flock. Mama baaed for him but he didn't answer her calls.

Greg looked up at Mama who was watching them from across the grass, her head sticking up from the flock. Her eyes smoldered at him. He looked away and returned his attention to the grass.

"She's not happy with me. None of them are. They probably all think I put you up to it."

"We need to figure out how to get through to them. How to get them to see the truth."

"Forget it. They're sheep. Even if they believed you and knew the truth, they still wouldn't leave the safety of the shepherd and the dog. It's a terrible thing being a sheep."

"Considering all that's happened, I still like being what I am."

"You like being at the bottom of the food chain?"

Bucky looked up and thought over the question for a long moment.

"I think it would be a terrible thing to have to kill other creatures just to eat. I don't know how predators can live with themselves, knowing they cause so much fear and suffering in others. I would much rather be a sheep with a clear conscience than some vicious meat eater. Personally, I think we sheep are the best of all the animals, even the humans. We don't harm anyone, we only help. We clear the fields, and give them fleece and milk for their cheese."

"And meat to eat."

"What a terrible thing to be a human and receive so much and turn around and harm us as they do."

"If I had the choice, I wouldn't be a sheep."

"What's wrong with being a sheep?"

"Better to eat than be eaten."

Bucky looked up at the shepherd smoking his cigarette and reading his book on the rock with Stevie at his feet.

"It's terrible that we're trapped here. It's a terrible thing knowing the truth and being unable to do anything about it."

"This is our curse. We're smart enough to know the truth but too dumb to do anything about it."

"We've got to do something."

"I admire you, Bucky. You tried to do something. It was a heroic thing. The fact that they wouldn't listen says more about them than you. It was their failing, not yours. They're all too dumb to see the truth. They deserve a leader like Papa."

"I just wish there was something we could do. A way out of here."

"You'll never convince sheep of something they don't want to know."

"Let's make a run for it, Greg. We can break from the flock and run for the hills."

"If we run, Stevie will come after us. He's too fast. Trust me. I've tried it."

"I wish there was some way out of this place."

"Do you really mean that?"

"I do."

"Maybe there is a way. Come. Follow me."

Greg walked through the high grass toward the fence. Bucky looked over his shoulder at the flock and then followed.

The Leap

Bucky followed Greg down a deer trail. They came to an outcropping piled with large boulders. Atop the rounded outcropping and between the boulders stood an old, twisted oak tree. Its thick trunk was bent sideways before twisting upward then curling and branching out asymmetrically in every direction.

A misty sun shower fell over the sunlit landscape as the two sheep made their way between the boulders and around the gnarled oak then down an embankment to a creek. The multi-colored arch of a huge rainbow stretched and bowed over the vineyards beyond the fence. In the distance, a dark wall of rain clouds hung ominously over the coastal range.

The creek bed was normally dry, but the heavy rains had filled it with swiftly flowing water that rushed over the rocky bottom.

Greg walked in the mud on the water's edge until he came to the barbed wire fence. The water flowed swiftly under the fence and down into a gully that bordered the vineyard. Green grass waved in the water, caught in the swift flow under the fence.

Greg jumped up the embankment and walked along the fence. Bucky followed him up. The two sheep followed the fence until Greg came to a stop. He looked around, searching the high grass.

"I stood here last summer and noticed how the fence dips here. Look there. See that rise? With a running start, a strong sheep could jump from the top of the rise and vault right over the fence."

Bucky studied the rise and the dip in the fence.

"And if a strong sheep got a running start and jumped over the fence, then what?"

"That sheep could follow the fence line to the mountains. Then it's a matter of climbing the mountains to Liberty Mountain. Once there, the strong sheep would be free."

"There's danger beyond the fence."

"Much danger. Coyotes. Bears. Mountain lions. Rattlesnakes. Wild dogs."

"Is that all?"

"Humans."

"When you were standing here last summer, why didn't you jump?"

"Because there's danger beyond the fence."

"That's what sheep say."

"The flock must stay together."

"The shepherd watches over us. The dog protects us."

"That's what sheep say."

Bucky walked around the rise. He looked up the slope and took two steps back.

"What are you doing?" Greg asked.

Bucky lowered his head and charged up the rise.

"Bucky!"

Bucky reached the top of the rise at a full gallop. He leaped from the top and soared through the air with his back straight, knees bent and nose pointed forward. He cleared the top strand of barbed wire and landed at a run on the other side. He slid on his hooves through the mud and skidded to a stop. He spun around, looked at Greg and smiled broadly.

"You were right. A strong sheep can jump right over the fence. What are you waiting for? Hurry up."

"I didn't think you'd actually do it," Greg said through the barbed wire.

"Get up there and jump over."

Greg looked over his shoulder at the rise and then at the barbed wire fence.

"I'm not sure I can jump it. I'm not as young as I used to be."

"Of course you can jump it. Now get up there, run as hard as you can, and jump."

Greg looked over at Bucky standing in the muddy road on the other side of the fence.

"Do you see any danger over there?"

Bucky looked around.

"Coyotes. Bears. Lions. Wild dogs. Danger everywhere. Now get up there and jump over."

"Fine."

Greg turned around and walked to the foot of the rise. He stood at the bottom for a long moment staring forward.

"You can do it."

"You sure are one crazy sheep."

Greg took two steps back, lowered his head and charged up the rise. He skidded to a stop at the top.

"You had it. What did you stop for?"

"I don't know about this, Bucky. We should head back to the flock before Stevie comes for us."

"It's too late now. How am I supposed to get back over? You were the one who talked me into this."

"But I didn't think you'd actually do it."

"Isn't this what you've always wanted? This is your chance to escape the flock. Now hurry up. Let's go find Zeus."

Greg walked back to the bottom of the slope. He scratched the ground with his front hoof, lowered his head and charged up the rise. He leaped from the top and soared through the air with back straight, knees bent and nose pointed forward. His front knees clipped the top strand of wire, sending him tumbling head over tail through the air.

He crashed onto the mud, landing on the back of his neck. He rolled over and over in the mud before finally sliding to a stop.

Bucky ran up to him.

Greg looked up at him from the mud, half dazed from the tumble.

"You're one crazy sheep," he said.

Bucky helped him onto his feet. The old sheep shook himself off and looked around.

"We're on the other side of the fence."

"We sure are," Bucky said.

"We've really done it now."

"If we follow the fence, we'll reach the mountains. What are you waiting for? Let's go. I bet Stevie's looking for us by now."

Bucky walked along the fence on the muddy road. Greg followed behind. On their left was an endless vineyard. Its rows ran parallel up and down the rolling hills. The woody, leafless grapevines branched like crosses on the trellises. Green grass grew high in the rows between the vines.

Greg was alert as he walked. He scanned left and right, swiveling his ears and quickly turning his head at the slightest rustle in the grass.

"Keep your eyes out for predators," he said.

Bucky led the way walking along the muddy road, clopping through the puddles.

"I must say," Bucky said. "I never wanted to leave the flock until last night. And now we've done it, Greg. We're going to Liberty Mountain to find Zeus and his wild flock."

"I've been dreaming about this for years," Greg said. "I can't believe we're actually on our way. It is exciting, if you think about it. No more Stevie. No more Bonehead. No more listening to stupid sheepisms day in and day out."

Bucky came to a sudden stop and stood motionless in the center of the road.

"What is it?"

"Do you hear that?"

"Is it wild dogs?"

"Run."

Bucky darted into the vineyard between the vines. Greg chased after him with terror in his eyes. As Greg ran down the row, he tripped on a pile of chopped grapevine cuttings hidden by the tall grass. Greg tumbled through the grass. He struggled in panic to get to his feet.

Bucky spun around and ran back to him.

"Greg."

Bucky looked up through the grass and trellises.

"Don't move a muscle."

The two sheep stood motionless under the vines.

The clop-clop-clop of hooves grew louder.

"Daddy, look there," a little girl said.

Rachel sat in the saddle on top of an enormous chocolate-colored horse. She had a cowboy hat on over her long brown hair and cowboy boots on her feet that were in the stirrups. Her horse looked monstrous to the two sheep who watched with wide eyes through the vines. The horse was only a few feet from them.

"What is it?" Rancher Dave asked from atop the horse behind her.

"There," she said.

Rancher Dave pulled his horse up alongside Rachel's.

"There, Daddy. Do you see them?"

"I sure do."

The Rabbit

"Up there in the rocks by that old oak tree," Rachel said.

"I see him. Look at the antlers on him."

"He's beautiful."

"And the doe," Rancher Dave said. "Look, there's another one."

As Rachel and her father watched the deer on the other side of the fence, her horse took the opportunity to nibble on the grass at the edge of the vineyard.

As the horse grazed, it caught sight of Greg and Bucky huddling between the vines.

"Shhh," Bucky said.

The horse watched the two sheep with its big eye as it ate.

"Please, Mr. Horse," Bucky whispered. "Don't give us away."

The horse winked, lifted its head and whinnied.

The stag on the other side of the fence bolted between the boulders. The two does followed.

"Let's go, Daddy. Race you back."

The horses with their riders trotted away down the muddy road.

Bucky and Greg remained motionless listening to the clop and splash of hooves grow fainter in the distance. They peeked their heads out from the vineyard.

"It looks clear," Bucky said. "Let's go."

The two sheep continued walking down the muddy road.

"Why do you suppose the horses allow the humans to ride on their backs?" Bucky asked.

"That's a good question. I don't suppose the horses like it. Yet they allow the humans to sit atop them."

"The horses are so much bigger than the humans. They're double the size, maybe triple. They're stronger and faster, yet the humans control them."

"It's a conundrum."

"A human is small and weak compared to a horse. Why don't the horses throw the humans off their backs and tell them they're not going to take it anymore or else they'll smash them with their hooves?"

"They should do that."

"Why don't they? I don't get it."

"Maybe horses are dumber than sheep."

"They need to stop letting the humans ride around on top of them. The humans can walk just like everyone else and shouldn't take advantage of animals like that. It's not right."

"Perhaps we shouldn't be hard on the horses for allowing the humans to ride around on their backs.

After all, there are three hundred of us sheep in the flock, and only one human and his dog control us. Why haven't we ever rebelled? We must be pretty feeble-minded ourselves."

"But a horse is so much bigger than a sheep."

"Look at all of us sheep unable to stand up to a single man and his dog."

"It's definitely a conundrum," Bucky said.

They walked along the fence for quite some time.

"Back in the corral, you never eat from the trough like the rest of us."

"Correct. I don't."

"Why not?"

"The humans put chemicals in the hay to make us docile and dumb, so we won't think about things."

"Really?"

"It's a fact."

"How do you know?"

"I just know."

"But how do you know?"

"Look how dumb all the sheep are."

As they walked they noticed up ahead that the fence veered south away from the mountains.

Greg stopped and looked through the fence.

"The mountains are on the other side of the fence," he said. "We're on the wrong side. If we keep following the fence, we'll never reach them."

"If you follow the fence, you'll reach Rancher Dave's house," a voice said.

Bucky and Greg turned to see a white-tailed rabbit standing on its hind legs on the other side of the road. Its nose twitched as it examined them.

"I've never seen sheep in these parts. What are a couple of sheep doing here away from your flock anyway?"

"We're going to Liberty Mountain," Bucky said. "We hear there's a flock of wild sheep that lives there."

"Wild sheep?" the rabbit asked. "That's an oxymoron, isn't it?"

"Have you heard of them?" Bucky asked.

"I'm afraid I haven't. If someone told me that a flock of wild sheep are running around up in the mountains, I'm sure I would've remembered it."

"Do you know how to get to the mountains, Rabbit?" Greg asked.

"Why, sure. That way." He pointed through the fence at the mountains in the distance. "Cross the river and head west and you'll reach them."

"We can't fit under the fence like you, Rabbit," Bucky said. "Do you know if there's a way through?"

"A way through?" The rabbit thought for a moment. "See the sycamore tree up there along the fence? It has a thick trunk that dips low over the ground and branches over the fence. I bet sheep like yourselves could jump up on the branch and walk over to the other side."

"Thank you, Rabbit," Bucky said. "Let's go, Greg."

"But I wouldn't cross the fence if I were you. The mountains are a long way off and there are predators around these parts. Coyotes, bobcats, eagles. They might take interest in a couple of fat sheep like yourselves."

"Mountain lions?" Greg asked.

"Yes, the mountains are full of them."

"Full of them, you say," Greg said.

"What are you doing out here, anyway? You have a shepherd to watch over you and a dog to protect you. Out here you're on your own. It's not safe around here. I should know. I might be small and fast and have a burrow to escape to, but nearly every day I have a close call. Coyotes chasing me or eagles and hawks trying to swoop down and snatch me. What chance do two fat sheep have out here? I bet every carnivore from the fence to the ocean caught your scent while you two loudly clopped along down this road. My guess is you'll both be eaten before you reach the river. My advice? You two should return to your flock. The wild is no place for a sheep."

"No, there is a place in the wild for us sheep," Bucky said. "We're not the helpless creatures you think we are. Come on, let's go, Greg."

Bucky turned away from the rabbit and walked down the road. Greg followed reluctantly.

"Don't say I didn't warn you."

The rabbit watched them for a moment and then hopped away through the fence.

The two sheep walked in silence in the afternoon light until they reached the thick white trunk of the sycamore. The base of the trunk split and branched into three large arms. One arm extended low over the ground and bent upward over the fence before dipping down low again and branching out over a ravine.

"Now what?" Greg asked.

"We jump up on the trunk and walk over it to the other side. Too easy."

"It doesn't look that easy to me. It's getting late, Bucky. I'm sure Stevie he has picked up our scent by now and is coming for us. Perhaps this was a bad idea. We should turn back before it gets dark. "

"Turn back? After we've come this far?"

"If we make it over the fence without falling off the top of that branch, we've still got a good ways to go before we reach the mountains. It will be dark soon. We'll have to spend the night away from the flock without the shepherd watching over us or the dog protecting us. And that rabbit said there are predators everywhere."

"That rabbit was just trying to scare us."

"Have you ever spent a night alone in the wild? Away from your Mama?"

"No," Bucky said. "Have you?"

"The rabbit was right. The wild is no place for sheep. Come on. Let's go back before it gets dark."

Bucky looked over his shoulder. "I sure miss Mama."

Greg turned and walked away from the tree.

Bucky followed him a few steps then stopped.

"No," he said.

"No?" Greg turned around. "Come on, Bucky. Let's get back to your Mama."

"I don't want to go back. I want to climb over the fence, cross the river and climb Liberty Mountain. I want to meet Zeus and his wild sheep. I want to be away from the humans. I want to be free."

"I do, too. But sheep who stray get eaten. I don't want to be eaten."

"You're speaking in sheepisms."

Greg's eyes looked left and right.

"And you hate sheepisms. If we cross the fence and journey to the mountains we could face many dangers. We might get eaten. But if we go back, sooner or later we'll be eaten by the humans, anyway. When have we had a chance like this, Greg? I think it's worth the risk."

"It's funny. This is what I've always wanted, to escape the flock and find Zeus. But now that we have the opportunity, I realize how foolish I've been. I'm just a sheep, Bucky."

"No. You're more than just a sheep. You're a mighty ram, strong and proud. A ram who thinks for himself. We can do this, Greg."

Bucky turned and leaped up onto the sycamore trunk. He looked down from the trunk at Greg.

"Let's journey to Liberty Mountain."

Greg looked up at him and shook his head.

"You're one crazy sheep."

Nightfall

Greg walked hesitatingly atop the thick sycamore branch that extended horizontally from the trunk. He carefully made his way between smaller leafy branches that shot vertically up from the larger branch. His knees wobbled as he attempted to maintain his balance.

Greg reached the highest point directly above the barbed wire fence. He stopped and looked down and his eyes went wide. They unfocused as he looked down at the ground below him.

"Don't stop," Bucky said. "And don't look down. A few more steps and you're over."

Greg closed his eyes, took a deep breath and stepped forward, carefully making his way down to where the branch dipped lower to the ground again.

"You made it."

He jumped down onto the grass.

"I thought you said it was going to be easy."

"It would've been if you hadn't looked down."

Greg pointed with his nose toward the mountains. "We'll keep walking that way through the hills until it gets dark. Then we'll have to find a safe place for the night."

The hills were smaller but steeper here and covered with scraggly oaks. Green lichen drooped like Spanish moss from the leafless branches. The two sheep made their way along the sides of the hills, stopping briefly every now and then to graze. They stayed off the ridges and avoided trees, boulders and brush where predators might lurk.

The sun was low in the western sky casting its afternoon light across the green hills.

"Everyone must've noticed we're missing by now," Bucky said.

"The shepherd probably hasn't yet," Greg said. "But I'm sure Stevie's onto us. The more distance we put between us and the fence, the better."

"What do you think the sheep are all thinking?"

"They're sheep. They only have a few thoughts in their heads."

"They're thinking there's danger beyond the fence," Bucky said.

"They're thinking the sheep that strays gets eaten," Greg said.

"The flock must stay together," Bucky said.

They walked across the hillsides as the sun fell lower in the western sky.

"I wonder if Mama's noticed we're missing."

"I'm sure she has. She's probably worried sick. I bet she blames me for leading you astray. And she hates me for it."

In front of them stood a large grove of enormous eucalyptus trees. The tall trees were well over a hundred feet high. The thick trunks were closely clustered together. The stand of trees stretched north and south for at least a mile in either direction.

"Do we go around them or through them?" Greg asked.

"The most direct route is to go through them. I can see sunlight through the leaves. I don't think the grove goes back that far. It shouldn't take long to walk through to the other side."

"Famous last words."

Bucky walked under the towering trees into the grove. Greg followed him in.

The thick tree trunks were smooth in places or else covered in long strips of peeling bark. The earth was wet and spongey and slicked black with decomposing leaves. Large strips of tree bark had fallen from the trunks and littered the ground. Ferns and tufts of grass grew here and there between the trees. Gusts of wind blew through the fluttering leaves at the tops of the branches.

They walked between the massive tree trunks and down an embankment. At the bottom, a stream of water flowed over the leaves and grass. They splashed across the stream in the twilight. Darkness was quickly descending as they climbed up the opposite side of the embankment. As they walked through the trees, an eerie silence fell over the grove. Bucky stopped and looked back at Greg who had a worried look on his face.

A yip-yip-yipping broke the silence.

"Coyotes."

The sheep stood dead in their tracks, their eyes darting and ears swiveling as they searched the darkening grove.

The yapping was coming from just outside the grove up ahead of them. Through the tree trunks, they caught sight of the lithe form of a coyote swiftly running through the grass sniffing at the air and at the ground in the fading light.

"He's caught our scent," Greg said.

"We better go back."

They turned around and quietly made their way down the embankment and back up the other side. More yapping came from where they had entered the grove.

"They're on both sides," Bucky said. "They're talking to each other."

Bucky and Greg walked parallel to the embankment, ears swiveling as the yaps called back and forth from both sides of the grove.

"Over here," Greg said.

Several large boulders formed an overhang on one side of the embankment. A fallen eucalyptus trunk was atop the boulders. Its branches draped over the big rocks. Greg backed in between the boulders and disappeared in the dark.

"We can hide in here."

Bucky walked under the overhanging rocks and pushed through the branches. He stood beside Greg. They looked out from their hiding place searching for movement and sound.

The dusk turned to dark. The two sheep shuddered at each yip and yap of the coyotes. The coyotes were in the grove now searching the leaves and the brush, moving swiftly and communicating.

"They're getting closer," Greg said.

"I count at least three of them."

"I count four. Sounds like a mother and her half-grown pups. They're excited. They've got our scent. Shouldn't be long until they find us."

The sheep stood staring out into the darkness. Their knees were shaking. Their bodies trembled with each yap.

"I'm sorry," Bucky said.

"Sorry for what?"

"I'm sorry for making you leave the flock. It was stupid to think we could make it to the mountains."

"I'm the one who should be sorry. I put you up to this. I'm old. I've lived a long life, longer than most sheep. For all the indignities I've suffered, it's still been a good life. If I die here now, it's at the end of my life. But you're young with your whole life ahead of you. I never should've put all these thoughts in your head about Liberty Mountain, Zeus and his wild flock. You should be back with the flock to fulfill your promise. I should have never filled your head with things that were better left unsaid. The rabbit was right. The wild is no place for a sheep. I'm sorry, Bucky. You should've listened to your Mama and stayed away from me."

The coyotes were close now, swiftly moving back and forth, zeroing in on the scent. Then they went quiet.

"I don't hear them," Bucky whispered. "Let's run for it."

"No. Don't move."

In front of them down by the water, the ghostly form of a coyote stalked quietly with its head low to the ground.

It stopped, held one front paw off the ground and sniffed at the air.

The coyote froze staring up the embankment. But it wasn't looking in the sheep's direction.

Suddenly, a loud crashing sound broke the silence. The coyote sprinted up the embankment and disappeared through the trees.

"What was that?" Bucky asked.

"Shhh."

The crashing grew louder. Something large was moving through the trees and brush. The crashing got closer and closer until it was right on top of them.

In the darkness, a large black bear lumbered down the embankment in front of them. It stopped at the bottom and splashed into the water. It dropped something into the water and sniffed at the air with its big black nose.

Counting Sheep

The bear splashed around in the water in the dark. It had something in its mouth.

The two sheep stood under the rocks and log, trembling as they watched the big animal.

The bear looked up from the water directly at the two sheep. A dead Canada goose hung limply from its mouth. The goose's long neck swung back and forth as water dripped from the carcass into the stream. The bear sniffed the air for a moment, turned, and lumbered up the other side of the embankment, disappearing into the darkness.

Bucky and Greg stood under the overhang with knees shaking.

"Is he gone?" Bucky asked.

"I don't hear anything."

"I think he's gone. And the coyotes, too."

They stood peering into the darkness from under the rocks. Shivers ran through them in waves.

"We should stay here for the night," Greg said.

"That's a good idea."

Wind rustled through the leaves. An owl hooted in the darkness. Then all was silent again.

"I'd never seen a bear before," Bucky said.

"Me neither."

"Do they eat sheep?"

"I believe they do. But that one already had his mouth full."

They stood silently under the overhang. Every now and then the wind rustled through the trees. The owl hooted. Stars twinkled above the treetops in the dark sky.

"Maybe the coyotes aren't coming back," Bucky said. "Or the bear."

"I should hope not. Get some sleep. At first light, I'm taking you back to the flock."

"But we've come so far."

"This was a fool's errand. It's true what they say. There is danger beyond the fence. Those who stray get eaten. The flock must stay together. We should've never left the flock. I see the error in my ways now. Your Mama misses you, Bucky. She must be worried sick. We need to get back."

"I sure miss Mama."

"We were lucky we weren't eaten tonight. But those coyotes will come back for us sooner rather than later. And now we know there's a bear running around. We belong with the flock where the shepherd watches over us and the dog protects us. The wild is no place for a sheep."

The owl hooted. The wind rustled through the leaves.

"Get some sleep," Greg said. "I'll keep watch."

"OK."

Bucky stared out into the darkness. He couldn't sleep. All the excitement of the day had left him in a state of high alert. After some time, he heard Greg breathing slowly and methodically. The old sheep had fallen soundly asleep.

Bucky watched and listened. His eyes and ears played tricks on him in the darkness and silence. Clumps of ferns and tufts of grass took the form of stalking coyotes. Rocks and logs became bears.

He missed his Mama dearly. He longed to see her.

He stood motionless in the darkness under the overhang watching and listening and reviewing the events of the day over and over in his mind. Coyotes and bears and rabbits and horses. Owls and eagles and bobcats and lions. His eyes grew heavy.

He was back in the pasture grazing next to Mama. The sky was a brilliant blue. The sun shone brightly on the green grass. The air was warm. The flock was all around him. He felt happy and content. The shepherd up on the hillside stood and whistled. Papa trotted to the shepherd as the dog ran around behind the flock and herded them up the hill. Papa rushed through the gate into the corral and buried his head in the trough. The sheep entered behind him and moved warily, waiting for Papa to eat his fill. Once they were all inside, the shepherd closed the gate. Several men jumped into the corral and began separating the sheep. Bucky was herded with the young rams toward a chute that led up into a trailer. The humans herded the sheep one by one up the chute. Bucky ran up it and leaped onto the metal floor of the trailer. From the back of the crowded trailer, he saw his mother in the corral with the flock. Her head stuck up from the flock as she baaed desperately for him. "We're going to greener pastures, Mama." He watched her calling for him as the trailer pulled away from the corral and bumped down the road. The back of the trailer dropped open and the sheep ran out onto the cement floor of a slaughterhouse. The floor was slick with blood. The butchered carcasses of dead sheep hung from hooks all around them. The sheep baaed in fear between the swinging carcasses. The slaughterhouse door swung open. A human wearing a bloody butcher's frock stood in the doorway holding a large knife. The human grabbed Bucky by the back of the neck with his hard hands. Bucky struggled and cried for his Mama. The human was too strong. The big man slid the knife under Bucky's throat.

Bucky awoke with a jolt in the darkness.

His sudden movement startled Greg.

"What? What is it? Are the coyotes back?"

"No coyotes. Just a bad dream."

The wind rustled through the leaves. Stars twinkled through the leaves and branches. Thousands and thousands of stars sparkled in the night sky above the swaying treetops.

Bucky stood motionless in the darkness.

"I don't want to go back to the flock. I want to keep going. I want to make it to the mountains and meet Zeus and his flock of wild sheep. I want to live free, Greg."

"I do, too. But those who stray get eaten. We learned the truth of that today. I'm not going to be responsible for getting you killed."

"Those who stray get eaten. But those who stay get eaten, too. We're still here, Greg, alive. We can make it. If it's all the same to you, I'd like to take my chances out here in the wild rather than go back and wait for the humans to come for me."

"I'm old, Bucky. But you're young with your whole life ahead of you. If we keep going, we'd be taking huge risks. There's a chance we won't make it. In all probability, we won't. We don't even know if Zeus is really up there. Like I said, I don't want to be responsible for getting you killed."

"I left the flock of my own free will. If anything, I dragged you along with me. I'm willing to take the risks. But I understand if you choose to go back."

"There are a hundred reasons to go back."

"There are just as many to keep going."

"I don't count that many."

"I can't go back and live with flock knowing all that I know. I can't go back and pretend everything is fine knowing that sooner or later the humans will come for me and butcher me and eat me. I can't live a lie when I know the truth."

"That's only three reasons."

"If you want to go back to the flock, I don't blame you."

"I'm going back. You should come back with me."

"I'm going to keep going. When the sun comes up, I will continue to the mountains."

"Are you sure about this?"

"I'm positive."

"You've made up your mind?"

"I have."

They stood in silence. Greg shook his head.

"You're one crazy sheep, you know that?"

"Crazy is staying with the flock waiting for the humans to come cut my throat."

Greg looked at him. "Get some sleep. You'll think more clearly in the morning."

The Storm

Night turned to dawn. A heavy fog rolled into the grove. Water droplets dripped from the trees and pattered onto the black mat of leaves that covered the wet ground.

The darkness slowly lifted revealing a misty morning. The trees faded into the mist in the diffuse light.

Bucky looked out from under the overhang, searching for any sign of bears or coyotes.

"Do you see anything?" Greg asked.

"All clear."

Bucky stepped down the muddy embankment. Greg followed. They both drank from the stream.

"Are you continuing this journey?" Greg asked.

"I am."

"I never should have told you about Zeus and his wild sheep. You should come back to the flock with me."

"I'm continuing on, Greg."

"Is there any changing your mind?"

"No. Please tell Mama I love her."

Greg stood in silence for a moment as the water flowed around his hooves.

"I'm not going back to the flock."

Bucky looked up from the stream and smiled.

"I'm glad you're coming with me, Greg. We're going to make it. You and me together. I know it."

"Hmph."

Bucky climbed up the embankment. He looked down at his friend.

"Come on. Let's go. We're wasting daylight."

"I'm coming with you, but don't be pushy about it."

Greg climbed up the embankment. The two sheep walked between the eucalyptus trees in the dense fog. The mist floated in wisps above them between the tree trunks.

They reached the edge of the grove and looked out into a clearing. The fog was so thick that visibility was only a few feet.

"I can't see a thing," Greg said.

"It's to our advantage. The fog gives us cover."

"It gives the coyotes cover, too."

They walked out into the damp grass and away from the grove. A wet chill was in the air. The fog dampened their wool as they walked.

The yip-yip-yip of several coyotes carried eerily through the fog. The two sheep stopped in their tracks and stood motionless.

They remained absolutely still for a long moment. But the coyotes didn't call out again.

Bucky motioned forward with his nose. "We'll have to move quickly and quietly."

Greg nodded. Worry was in his eyes.

They reached the edge of the clearing and began climbing a hill.

They followed the hillsides traversing one hill after the other moving quickly and quietly. The hills became steeper, more rugged and more tightly spaced. Fog floated through the trees. The oak trees were smaller here and the groves more dense. Water droplets dripped from the green lichen that drooped from the ends of the leafless branches.

Greg's pace slowed and he breathed heavily as they climbed the hillsides. Bucky stopped and waited for him on one of the steeper slopes.

Greg caught up to him and they walked side by side.

"Nature is beautiful," Bucky said as they walked, "but cruel. Cats eating mice. Hawks eating squirrels. Coyotes trying to eat us. I wish things weren't this way. Living creatures trying to eat each other. If it were up to me, animals wouldn't eat other animals."

"It is what it is."

"At least we sheep don't harm other living things."

"We eat the grass. I'm sure the grass doesn't appreciate it."

They made their way through arroyos and up cliffs. They wound around more hills, always scanning the terrain for danger while avoiding any potential hiding places where predators might lurk. They walked for hours in the cold fog.

Around noontime the sun finally burned through the haze. The sunshine shone down through breaks in the dark layer of low hanging clouds.

A pop-pop-pop carried through the hills. Bucky and Greg stopped at the sound. The cracks and pops repeated in the faraway distance.

The two sheep started walking again. They had heard these faraway pops of gunfire many times before, especially during the summer months. The pops and cracks and rat-tat-tats, and sometimes loud booms, were the normal background sounds of life in these hills. The sheep never paid the sounds much mind.

Bucky and Greg followed a muddy deer trail that led through chaparral that covered the backside of a hill.

"Keep your eyes and ears open," Greg said. "I saw coyote scat and tracks back there."

Bucky turned and looked at Greg as they walked down the trail.

"Do you remember that night back in the corral when the coyote had me and you came and stomped him?"

"How could I forget?"

"I've been thinking."

"Uh oh."

"Both of us are bigger than any coyote. If those coyotes come for us, I don't think we should run. I think we should stand our ground and stomp them. We should fight them."

"We're sheep. Our instincts tell us to run. The only reason I didn't that night was because there was nowhere to run to."

"Greg. Both of us are big strong rams. We're bigger than them. You and me together, I think we can take on any scraggly old coyotes."

Greg walked along in silence for a moment.

"You know what I think?" he asked.

"What?"

"I think you're one crazy sheep."

The wind picked up and the temperature dropped as they wound their way through the chaparral. The sun disappeared behind the darkening clouds. The two sheep reached the bottom of the hill and walked through another arroyo. A cold drizzle began to fall.

The wind blew harder. It whipped at the trees. Gusts of wind blew raindrops across the arroyo in waves.

Greg and Bucky walked side by side as the rain drenched them.

"We should take cover," Greg said.

"We should keep moving. I want to make it to the river."

Greg shivered as he walked. "In all my years, I've never seen a winter like this. We've had dry winters and wet winters. Last year we got quite a bit of rainfall, but this year we've had more rain than I ever remember. More rain than all the past years combined. It's as if nature is trying to make up for its past shortfalls all in one winter."

"I'd be happy if it never rained again."

The wind was howling now. The rain fell in sheets. The heavy raindrops pelted their skin and faces. Rivulets of water rushed down the hillsides and gullies.

The two sheep plodded through deep puddles in the pounding rain. The gusts of wind blew so hard that they had to stop and brace themselves before continuing to walk again.

They climbed a steep hill, slipping in the mud as water rushed around their hooves. They reached the crest feeling cold and tired and drenched to the bone. They huddled under an oak tree.

"Let's stop, Bucky," Greg said over the roar of the storm. "Let's wait for a break in the rain."

"Look," Bucky said.

To the south across the arroyo a coyote stood atop the crest of a hill. They could see its form on the hilltop—a predatory silhouette against the rain swept sky. The canine form disappeared and reappeared behind sheets of rain.

"Down there," Greg said, pointing in the opposite direction. "The river."

Below them, through the roaring rain, they saw a swollen river winding across a flat plain. The river had overflowed its banks. It was a roiling torrent of muddy water. White foam collected against half-submerged brush caught in the fast current.

They looked back at the hill where the coyote stood. They watched it through sheets of rain as it trotted along the hilltop and then dashed down the hill.

"He's been tracking us," Greg said. "He's coming for us."

"We'll have to cross the river to reach the mountains. Maybe he won't follow us across."

"The river looks wide. And angry. I've never seen a river so wide."

"We'll have to swim across."

"Bucky, I can't swim."

The River

Bucky and Greg made their way in haste down the hillside. They slipped and slid on the wet grass and in the mud as the rain pounded down.

They hurried across a grassy field. The wind and rain whipped at the grass and lashed their skin. They reached a gravel road filled with puddles that overflowed with rainwater. They crossed the road and picked their way through brush and between small trees. They reached the riverbank and looked down at the roiling water. The muddy water churned and swirled and surged against the banks.

A large section of the opposite bank collapsed into the churning water.

"The river is too wide here," Bucky yelled over the roar of the pounding rain. "There must be a narrower section where we can cross."

He looked up and down the river examining the banks. Rafts of sticks and leafy branches floated down the river, bobbing up and down in the swiftly moving current.

"Look," Greg yelled over the din. "On the hill."

A lone coyote stood atop the hill where the two sheep had been standing only moments before.

The coyote ran down the hillside behind sheets of pouring rain.

Bucky turned and looked down from the bank at the swiftly flowing water. "You know what?" he yelled as the rain ran down his face and nose. "I don't know how to swim either."

"How hard could it be? I think you just kick your legs and keep your nose above the water."

"The river is too wide here and the current too fast. We need to find a narrower section."

The coyote was at the bottom of the hill now. It loped across the field toward them.

"It's no use running," Bucky said. "He'll be on us soon. I say we stand and fight. There's two of us and one of him."

"Look," Greg said, pointing with his nose up the hill.

Two more coyotes stood in the rain at the crest. They ran back and forth atop the hill, then raced down the hillside in the rain.

"Three against two," Bucky said.

"I count five."

Two more coyotes appeared atop the hill.

"Every coyote in the hills must've caught wind of us," Greg said. He turned and looked down the riverbank at the roiling water.

The first coyote loped across the gravel road splashing through the puddles.

Greg leaped forward off the bank and dropped several feet through the air before plunging into the muddy water.

"Greg!"

Greg disappeared under the water for several seconds before breaking the surface a few yards down from the bank. The current had him and was pulling him rapidly downstream. He desperately attempted to keep his nose above the water, kicking hard with his legs. The current rapidly pulled him out toward the center of the river. He spun around and around with his nose held up above the water as he gasped for air. He bobbed up and down in the rapids as the current pulled him away and then pulled him underwater.

"Greg!"

Bucky ran along the bank trying to keep up with his friend. He jumped over boulders, crashed through brush and leaped over logs.

He jumped over a fallen tree that jutted out into the current. His hooves landed hard on the edge of the wet bank, which gave way underneath him. Bucky fell sideways as the bank collapsed. He splashed into the frigid water, pulled down with the muddy bank that dissolved in the surging current. He was completely submerged, pulled down deeper and deeper by the strong undertow. He kicked his legs as hard as he could, struggling for the surface, desperate for air. He felt himself drowning as he was spun around and around by the violent current. Panic set in as his lungs ached for air.

His nose broke the surface. He gasped air into his mouth, coughing and choking. The current pulled him up and down in the swift flow. He kicked with his legs in a desperate attempt to keep his head above water.

Greg was several yards in front of him being rapidly pulled by the surging current.

Further down the river, an oak tree had fallen from the bank. Its trunk and branches extended out to the center of the river. Water crashed and surged over it. Greg smashed into the trunk and desperately tried to seize the branches with his hooves.

Bucky kicked hard attempting to ride the current to the tree.

Greg's head was pulled underwater beneath the tree branches.

Bucky was moving so fast with the current that he feared crashing too hard into the tree trunk. He smashed against the hard, rough bark. The impact stunned him. He felt as though the force of the collision had cracked his ribs. The powerful undercurrent pulled him down under the tree trunk. The two sheep were tangled in the branches under the water.

Bucky felt kicks from Greg's hard hooves. He sank his teeth into Greg's hide and held on. He kicked free from the branches. Both sheep were washed under the tree and rapidly away, swirling around deep beneath the surface, crashing into rocks and dragging over the mud of the riverbed.

Bucky's head broke the surface. His teeth were still clasping onto Greg's wool.

They were being pulled toward a bend in the river where the water flowed up and over the flooded riverbank and through a grove of oaks. The river flowed rapidly around the tree trunks. They were no longer near the river's fast-flowing center. Bucky felt his hooves kicking against the bottom.

He kicked hard for the shallows still holding onto Greg with his teeth.

He sunk his hooves in the mud as the water washed up and over him. He backed up toward the shore tugging at Greg's hide. He pulled until he was knee-deep in the rushing current. With all his might he yanked Greg to the shallows. He pulled and tugged until Greg was lying on his side in the mud, the water flowing around him. Greg lifted his head out of the water and gasped for air, coughing and choking.

Bucky pulled him onto the muddy shore. The rain came down in sheets, pelting the water that ran between the trees.

A coyote ran up and down the opposite bank, yipping and yapping at the sight of the two sheep across the river. Four more coyotes leaped and jumped through the brush and joined the first. The coyotes ran up down the bank searching for a place to cross. The first coyote leaped from the bank into the current. It paddled determinedly with its nose out of the water. The swift current pulled it downstream.

"Get up, Greg," Bucky said over the roar of the river and rain.

Greg lay on his side in the mud as the rain pelted him. He was breathing heavily, his face in the mud. He looked up with one eye at Bucky standing over him.

"Who knew?" Greg said. "Sheep can swim."

He smiled, the side of his face still pressed against the mud.

"Get up," Bucky said. "The coyotes are crossing the river."

Bucky nudged his friend with his nose. Greg hesitated for a moment, then struggled to his feet, his knees wobbly as Bucky steadied him.

The two sheep walked into the brush and through a forest of oaks. They climbed over logs and rocks as they walked through the high grass between the trees.

They were exhausted. Bucky plodded forward. He turned to see Greg standing motionless. Greg's head was down. Rainwater streamed over his face and down his nose. His knees gave out. He collapsed in the high grass.

Bucky walked up to him and sniffed him. Greg's eyes were open, staring into nothingness.

Bucky stood over him. He could barely stand himself.

The tree branches above danced in the wind as the rain poured down. They could walk no farther.

Bucky's body was heavy. His legs were weak. He lay down in the grass next to his motionless friend as the rain poured down from the dark sky.

Pigs

A lone songbird sang from a treetop. The intermittent warble of the birdsong broke the silence. Then the grove fell silent again.

Beams of golden sunlight filtered down through the oak branches. Bucky lay on his side in the grass. The inside of his eyelids glowed red from the warm sunlight on his face. He opened his eyes without lifting his head. He lay still in the sunbeam, listening to the warble of the birdsong.

Greg slept deeply next to him in the grass.

Bucky lifted his head and then kicked up onto his feet. He was in an oak forest that ran parallel to both sides of the river for several miles.

The sky above the treetops was clear and powder blue, the kind of vibrant blue that comes only after a night of rain.

Bucky scanned the forest with his eyes and swiveled his ears searching for any sign of coyotes. Detecting none, he lowered his head and sniffed at Greg.

Greg opened one eye and looked up at Bucky. "I thought I was dead."

"There's danger beyond the fence."

"That's what sheep say."

Greg struggled to his feet, groaning and rolling his eyes with each movement.

"We better get moving," Bucky said. "The more distance we put between us and the river the better."

Bucky began to walk between the tree trunks. Greg followed, moaning and groaning with each step. Bucky felt the aches and pains, too. He looked at his friend hobbling behind him, then stopped and began nibbling at the green grass that grew in tufts between the trees. Greg walked up to Bucky and began to graze.

"Oh, yeah," Greg said. "This grass is good."

"It really is."

They walked from tuft to tuft beneath the trees, grazing each tuft down to the stems. They took their time, walking and grazing in the shadows and filtered sunlight of the morning.

"Look at the ground," Greg said. "Someone's been destroying the forest floor."

All around them the earth had been torn up and uprooted. The ground between the oaks had been dug up, overturned and rutted, creating a wet muddy mess.

Bucky and Greg walked through the mud of the destroyed forest floor. Muddy puddles filled the holes and ruts.

"Who could've caused such destruction?" Bucky asked.

"Destruction?" a voice said from behind them. "I call it creative landscaping."

Bucky and Greg spun around to see a giant feral pig much larger than themselves standing behind them. It had black skin and bristly black hair. Sharp white tusks stuck out from its porcine snout. A large bristly hump jutted upward from its shoulders.

"It's an improvement if you ask me."

"Yes, I would say so," another voice said. "Quite an improvement."

"Definitely an improvement."

"Creative landscaping, indeed."

The two sheep were suddenly surrounded by at least a dozen large, black pigs. The pigs snorted and sneezed and rutted around in the mud.

The first pig to have spoken was far larger than the rest. The big boar stepped forward in the mud and examined Bucky and Greg.

"Who are you?" he asked.

"I'm Bucky and this is Greg."

"I'm Rolo, king of the pigs."

He sniffed them with his muddy snout. He turned to the others.

"Sheep," he said.

He turned back to Bucky and Greg. "We've never seen sheep in these parts. What are two fat sheep doing so far away from your flock?"

"We're on a journey to the mountains to find Zeus and his flock of wild sheep," Bucky said. "They live on Liberty Mountain. Have you heard of them?"

"A journey, you say? To the mountains?"

"Yes. Have you heard of Zeus?"

"Wild sheep, you say? But you don't look wild. You look… domesticated."

"Yes, we are from a flock across the river, watched over by a shepherd and a dog. We escaped."

"Gone feral, have you?"

"Feral?"

"Do you see that we look different from ordinary pigs?"

"You are very different."

"We're leaner, more muscular, fiercer."

"Your tusks are much larger and sharper than an ordinary pig's."

"The wild does that to an animal. The wild turns us feral and fierce. Fat and domestic won't survive here for long."

"Have you heard of a flock of sheep that live in the mountains?"

The big boar sniffed Bucky again with his snout.

"I find it highly unlikely that sheep live wild in the mountains."

"Why's that?"

"Because Puma eats everything that moves up there."

The big boar walked around them. Bucky and Greg were completed surrounded by the pigs that watched them with glistening eyes.

"Let me give you some advice. Go back to your flock. You'll never make it to the mountains. You'll be eaten before you ever reach them."

"Who's Puma?"

"Why, he's the most fearsome predator from here to the ocean."

"Fearsome," said a female pig.

"He's fearsome all right," said another.

"Very fearsome."

"The fearsomest."

"More fearsome than a pack of coyotes?" Bucky asked.

The big pig laughed and the others joined in.

"Much more fearsome. More fearsome than legions of coyotes."

"He lives in the mountains?" Greg asked.

"He lives in a mountain lair filled with bones. All kinds of bones. Piles of them."

"Rabbit bones."

"Turkey bones."

"Deer bones."

"Elk bones."

"Pig bones."

The female pig began to weep.

"Puma ate my little Wally just two months ago. My little Wally. My poor little Wally."

"Sheep bones?" Bucky asked.

"As I said, I haven't seen any sheep in these parts. But I'm sure old Puma would love a sample."

"Mmm. Mutton."

"Mutton chops."

"Lamb chops."

"Lamb stew."

"Lamb sausage."

"Shish kebabs."

"Roast leg of lamb."

"Smoked mutton leg with all the trimmings."

The big pig sniffed at Bucky with his muddy snout. The female pig sniffed at Greg from behind.

"Mmm. Mutton."

"Well, we better get going. It's been nice chatting with you. Come on, Greg."

Bucky and Greg tried to walk away but they were surrounded. The pigs blocked their path.

"Going so soon?"

Bucky tried to push past them. The female pig sniffed at his rump with her muddy snout, then sunk her teeth into his haunches.

"Ouch. Hey, what are you doing?"

"Just a little nibble."

"Stop. Hey. Knock it off. Cut it out. What do you think you're doing? Come on, now. We herbivores need to stick together."

"Herbivores?"

The big boar smiled. Drool dripped from his tusks. "But we're not herbivores. We're omnivores."

"What's an omnivore?"

The pigs were smiling deviously. They had a hungry look in their eyes.

"Omnivores eat everything."

"Mmm. Mutton."

"What do we do now?" Greg whispered.

Bucky lifted his head above the pigs and stared back into the forest. He widened his eyes.

"Puma!" he yelled.

"Puma?" the big pig said.

"Puma!"

"PUMA!"

The pigs squealed and ran in every which direction, kicking up mud as they bolted through the trees.

"Puma!" Greg yelled running with them.

"Greg!" Bucky said running behind him. "Follow me. There's no Puma."

"There's no Puma? Right, there's no Puma."

Greg turned and ran after Bucky. The two sheep raced through the oaks away from the squealing pigs. They ran to the edge of the forest and out onto a grassy field. They sprinted up a hill and down the backside and then up and down another. They reached the top of the next hill and stopped and fell down panting in the grass.

"There was no Puma," Greg said.

"Nope."

"Did you see the look in their eyes when you yelled Puma?"

"Did you see how fast they ran?"

The two sheep laughed.

"You should've seen your eyes."

Bucky and Greg lay in the grass laughing.

"You're one crazy sheep."

They rested under the morning sun.

"Hey, Bucky. I'm concerned about Puma."

"Puma is the least of our concerns now." Bucky got up onto his feet. "The pigs have probably figured out there's no Puma. They'll be coming after us. We better get moving."

Greg groaned.

Bucky looked to the west. Liberty Mountain loomed large against the blue sky.

"It's not far now."

The Kit Fox

Bucky and Greg walked up and down the hills on high alert for any sign of mountain lions, coyotes or feral pigs. The country here was much more rugged with steeper hills, rocky cliffs and large oaks.

Morning turned to afternoon. They walked quietly seeing no signs of wildlife other than turkey buzzards circling high overhead or the occasional hawk.

The hard climbing was wearing them out. They stopped here and there to graze and drink water from puddles. Bucky often had to stop and wait for Greg who trudged along slowly behind him.

They reached the top of a hill and looked down the other side where a large sloping plain stretched out before them.

"We'll have to cross the plain," Bucky said. "There's a lot of fresh grass down there."

"Yes, but it's wide open ground. We'll be very visible to all around when we cross it."

"But any predators will be visible as well. We'll be able to see them coming from far away."

"Perhaps."

"We'll waste too much time if we try to go around. I say we cross straight through."

"I agree. I've had enough hill climbing today."

The two sheep walked down the hillside and out onto the flat expanse of green.

The breeze washed and rolled over the grass in waves. They walked through the tall grass, occasionally stopping to graze while keeping a wary eye out for prowlers.

Small craters pockmarked much of the plain. Water from the rains filled the depressions. Beneath the grass, the floor of the plain was littered with small twisted shards of metal shrapnel.

Bucky stopped and drank from a puddle at the bottom of crater. The sun glinted against the shallow water that was cool and clear against the muddy bottom. Fairy shrimp swam beneath the surface. The tiny pinkish creatures were nearly translucent. They had elongated bodies, black eyes on stalks and thin antennae. They swam upside down in the shallow pool using dozens of tiny legs that oscillated in waves up and down their thoraxes.

Bucky observed the fairy shrimp until Greg clopped into the pool and splashed his head down and gulped in the cool water.

"Be careful. There are living creatures in the pool."

"Bugs?"

"I don't think so." Bucky looked closely at them. "What a strange place to call home. One sunny day could dry up this puddle and their home will be gone."

"I don't see anything." Greg looked closely into the water. "My eyes aren't as good as they used to be."

They continued on through the billowing grass. A large rusted hulk became visible ahead of them.

"What is it?" Bucky asked

"Don't know and don't care. Let's stay away from it."

Bucky walked toward the hulk.

"Let's see what it is."

"Not a good idea."

Bucky walked closer to it while Greg kept his distance.

The metal hulk sat on old rusted caterpillar treads. A large turret was atop it. A cannon jutted out from the turret. Grass grew up between the treads and weeds grew along the metal top and sides. The hulk was an ancient tank, full of holes and blast marks across its metal armor. Some of the holes were quite large. The metal around the holes was twisted, sharp and rusty.

Bucky looked up at the tank, walked around it and studied it. Greg walked up to him hesitatingly.

"What could it be?" Bucky asked.

"It looks like some kind of human vehicle or machine. But it's seen better days. It doesn't look like it's moved from this spot in quite some time."

The two sheep stood under the tip of the cannon and looked up at it.

"What do you suppose it's for?" Bucky asked.

"It's a gun," a voice echoed from inside the cannon.

The two startled sheep jumped back.

"It speaks!" Greg said.

A small canine head peeked up from atop the turret. It had a pointy nose, dark eyes and massively oversized pointy ears. The little creature disappeared back behind the turret.

The two sheep stepped forward craning their necks trying to see atop the tank.

"Boo!"

The sound echoed loudly out of the cannon, again startling the two sheep who jumped back with eyes wide.

Laughter erupted from the cannon.

"Who are you?" Bucky demanded.

The little head popped up from atop the turret.

"The question is, who are you?"

"I'm Bucky and this is Greg. We're two sheep who've escaped our flock."

"Interesting."

The creature jumped down from the turret and walked along the metal side of the tank. It was as small as a house cat and had a rusty gray coat and a long, furry tail, black at the tip.

"What are you?" Greg asked. "Some kind of midget coyote?"

"I'm no dirty coyote. My name is Carlos. I'm a kit fox."

"Pleased to meet you, Carlos," Bucky said.

"Why are you sheep out here away from your flock, wandering the wilderness?"

"We're on a journey to the mountains to meet Zeus, the leader of a flock of wild sheep," Bucky said. "Have you heard of Zeus and his wild sheep?"

"Wild sheep? Never heard of such a thing."

"They live there on Liberty Mountain."

The fox looked over his shoulder at the coastal range. A wall of fog was held back by the mountains, but billowed around Liberty Mountain, which jutted up above the range.

"Seems implausible."

The little animal walked closer to the sheep and stood in profile on the side of the tank looking down at them.

"Now I have a question for you. You came from the other side of the river, correct? Have you seen other kit foxes on your journey?"

"I can't say that we have," Bucky said. He looked at Greg who shrugged his shoulders.

Carlos looked disappointed.

"What's wrong?" Bucky asked.

"I haven't seen another of my kind in years. I think I may be the last of my breed."

"There must be other foxes around."

"I think not. The humans have overrun much of the land. And coyotes eat our prey. They chase me and constantly harass me. I think maybe these are the last days of my kind. For all I know, I'm the last kit fox. At least in these parts, anyway."

"I hate those coyotes," Bucky said.

"We better get moving," Greg said. "It's late afternoon. It'll be dark soon."

"Be careful. There are humans about. Lots of them."

"We haven't seen any," Bucky said.

"They're up in the woods in large numbers. They've been driving down the roads in their vehicles and tromping through the hills."

"We'll keep an eye out," Greg said.

"If we see any other kit foxes, we'll let them know you're looking for them," Bucky said.

"Greatly appreciated."

Above them high in the sky a bright white light flickered and flared and trailed a plume of white smoke. The flare hung from a small white parachute that coasted downward on the breeze.

"Uh oh," the kit fox said.

In the distance on a ridge on the far side of the plain, mortar tubes were lined up in a row. Soldiers dropped mortar rounds into the tubes. The tubes emitted hollow thump, thump, thumps as the rounds shot out and upward.

The sheep and the fox strained their eyes at the distant ridge.

"I see movement up there," Carlos said. "Humans."

"I don't see anything," Greg said.

"Strange hollow thumping sounds," Carlos said.

"I heard it, too," Bucky said.

A whistling sound above them increased in amplitude. A shocking explosion rocked the earth, blasting open a large crater in the ground and throwing dirt, grass and shrapnel into the air. The blast wave hit the sheep like a sledge hammer, knocking them to the ground and stunning them.

Bucky shook his head. The wind was knocked out of him. His ears rang loudly. His vision was blurry. He looked up from the ground and gasped in air as he tried to get his bearings. Another whistle shrieked down from above. The earth exploded again. The blast wave slammed against them with a crack.

Bucky ran up to Greg and pulled him up to his feet with his teeth.

Another whistle shrieked in the sky.

"Run!"

The two sheep sprinted in panic through the grass. The tank exploded behind them in a burst of metal and flame.

Sheepish

Mortar rounds whistled down from the sky and impacted with bone-crushing whumps. Bucky and Greg ran in terror as the powerful blast waves smashed against them, spun them around and knocked them down, sending them tumbling and sliding across the grass. Geysers of earth shot up around them. They scrambled and ran as mud, dirt and clumps of grass splattered against them.

The two sheep ran to the end of the plain and sprinted up a hillside. They ran hard between the trees, up and down the rugged hills, crashing through the brush and leaping over bushes, logs and rocks.

Bucky sprinted like a greyhound until he came to the realization that he was running alone. He had outrun Greg, or else his friend had been pulverized in one of the powerful explosions. Bucky slid to a stop, breathing hard, his heart pounding. His ears rang loudly. His head hurt.

He turned panting heavily and searched between the trees for any sign of his friend.

Greg ran at a full gallop between the tree trunks. His eyes were wide with terror. His tongue flapped from the side of his mouth as he ran.

Greg barreled past Bucky and kept going. Bucky turned and chased after him through the trees.

Greg galloped down a hillside, jumped over a narrow gully and then scaled a dirt cliff in several frantic leaps. He reached the top of the cliff and ran straight up the steep hillside.

Bucky caught up to him and ran alongside him.

"Greg. You can stop now."

Greg looked over at Bucky with wide eyes, his tongue flapping from the side of his mouth as he ran. He ran a few more yards, then slowed and stopped. He breathed hard, panting and wheezing, trying to catch his breath.

"We're far enough away. I think we're safe now."

"I thought the world was coming to an end," Greg gasped.

"I did, too."

They stood under the trees until Greg's breathing slowed.

"Come on," Bucky said. "Let's head down the hill and find some water."

The two sheep walked down into a narrow arroyo where clear, cold water flowed through a channel carved between the hills. They drank and drank until their bellies were full.

The sun was low on the western horizon. The clouds in the west were aglow in brilliant pink, red and orange. Sunbeams shot up from behind the mountains and radiated through the clouds.

"I can't walk another step," Greg said.

"We can bed down in the grass on the hillside."

The two sheep climbed halfway up the next hill and lay down in the high grass.

The fiery colors of the sunset slowly faded. The clouds became black silhouettes against the gray sky as the sunlight dissipated. The sky faded to black.

The two sheep sat silently watching and listening over the grass.

"It's been one near-death experience after another," Greg said.

"I've been worried about coyotes. Not about the earth exploding beneath our hooves."

"I'm never going back that way again."

"Me neither."

"First the coyotes try to eat us. Then the river tries to drown us. Then the pigs try to eat us. Now the earth explodes around us. It's true what they say. There is danger outside the fence. Much danger."

"I can't deny it. But somehow we're still alive."

"I don't know how much longer our luck will last."

"We're going to make it, Greg."

"All these years I've thought the sheepisms everyone repeated were a bunch of bunk. But I'm learning they're true. The shepherd really did watch over us. The dog really did protect us. The flock should stay together. Maybe I'm not as smart as I thought I was. Maybe I've been the dumb one."

The sky was dark now. Twinkling stars appeared in the firmament. Bucky and Greg looked up at the starry sky.

"The shepherd watched over us, the dog protected us and the flock stayed together so that someday the humans could come take us away, slaughter us and eat us."

"That's a sheep's fate in life. To be eaten, one way or another."

"I can't accept that."

"At least with the flock we were safe."

"Don't lose heart, Greg."

The two sheep sat in silence in the dark as the wind blew softly over the grass.

Greg chewed his cud as he looked out at the stars. He belched.

"It's going to be a cold one tonight," he said.

"How do you know?"

"My knees are aching."

"I think two more days of walking and we'll reach Liberty Mountain. We're getting close, Greg. We're going to make it. We're going to meet Zeus and his flock."

"The kit fox hadn't heard of wild sheep living on Liberty Mountain. Neither had the pigs. Nor the rabbit."

"But the ground squirrel. He'd heard of a flock of sheep in the mountains."

"A flock of hundreds. Sheep as big as horses with giant antlers."

"Maybe living in the wild changed them. Like it did to the pigs."

"We're pinning our hopes on the word of a squirrel."

"I don't think he would make something like that up. They've got to be there."

"Maybe. But Bucky, there's much danger in the wild. There are many ways for a sheep's life to come to a quick end. Many years have passed since Zeus

147

left the corral. If somehow we reach Liberty Mountain without getting eaten by mountain lions, coyotes or feral pigs, or dying from drowning or explosions, or who knows what else, there's a good chance Zeus and his wild flock won't be there."

"No. I don't believe that. I can't believe we've come all this way and risked so much for nothing. I know he's there. I can feel it."

The edge of the moon crested a distant ridge of hills. They watched as the moon slowly rose above the ridgeline.

The bright disk cast silver moonlight against Greg's dark face, illuminating his big eyes. He looked over at his young friend and studied him in the moonlight.

"I'm not as certain as you," he said. "Maybe Zeus is there, maybe not. But I'll continue on this journey with you, my friend. Perhaps we'll reach Liberty Mountain without getting eaten. Then we'll know for sure."

Bucky smiled. "We'll make it."

A chill wind blew down the hillside. The sheep sat silently in the grass gazing at the moon and stars. The temperature was dropping rapidly.

The rumbling of diesel engines carried through the darkness. In the distance, a line of white lights moved between the hills. The rumble of engines grew louder as the lights grew closer.

"Human vehicles," Greg said.

The white headlights appeared and disappeared as a convoy of trucks rumbled over a gravel road that wound between the hills. The lights got closer and the engines louder as the convoy neared the two sheep. Bucky and Greg hunkered down low in the grass as the convoy approached and then disappeared behind the hill across the gully.

"There are many of them," Greg said.

The red taillights of the trucks appeared on the other side of the hill as the vehicles rumbled away in the darkness.

"Where do you think they're going?" Bucky asked.

"Who knows? But the kit fox said the humans are in the hills in large numbers. I'm sure it was the humans that caused the explosions that almost killed us."

"I hope that kit fox made it off that metal wreck before the humans blew it up."

"Doubtful. But I hope so, too."

Soldiers

The grass was blanketed by a crust of frost. An icy mist clung to the hillsides and filled the gullies. The frigid dawn air pierced through their wool into their skin and bones.

Bucky and Greg lay in the tall grass waiting for the sun to rise up and warm them from the biting cold.

The darkness turned to twilight which was slowly overtaken by the light of the rising sun. Sunbeams broke through the mist and sparkled on the frosty grass.

The two sheep remained prostrate in the grass as the sun slowly burned away the mist and melted the frost. Steamy puffs shot from their nostrils with each exhalation of the frigid air.

Greg yawned and stretched his neck.

"Oh, my aching bones," he groaned.

"Your aching bones were right. It was freezing last night."

"They're never wrong."

They struggled to their feet and then quietly grazed on the hillside where the sun had melted away the frost.

"Shhhh," Bucky said.

He pointed up the hillside with his nose.

A flock of wild turkeys emerged from the brush. At least twenty of the large birds were walking down the hillside pecking at the ground beneath the grass. The big turkeys had long legs, black feathers that were speckled with gray at the wings, and red featherless heads.

"Maybe they know where Zeus and his flock are," Bucky said.

"A bunch of turkeys?"

"It couldn't hurt to ask."

Bucky raised his head and baaed to the turkeys.

A big tom turkey with a long feathered tail stood up with head erect. It looked rapidly left and right. The red wattle on its throat flapped vigorously as it let out a loud, "Gobble, gobble, gobble, gobble, gobble."

Bucky baaed again.

"Gobble, gobble, gobble, gobble, gobble."

"Baaaaa."

"Gobble, gobble, gobble, gobble, gobble."

"Would you two shut up? Every coyote for miles around can hear you."

The big tom turned and ran with long strides back into the brush. The other turkeys disappeared into the brush behind him.

"They were no help," Bucky said.

"What did you expect? They're turkeys."

"And we're sheep."

"A sheep talking to a turkey. Now there's an intellectual conversation."

They grazed lazily in the misty morning air before setting out and continuing on their trek up and down the hills.

They reached the bottom of a hill and came to a gravel road. Bucky looked up and down the road through the mist. He hesitatingly stepped out onto the gravel.

"Come on. It's clear."

The two sheep walked out onto the road.

A quail darted out from the brush and ran across the road a few yards from the sheep. A curving plume of feathers hung over the running quail's head. Its little legs moved rapidly under its round body as it ran. A covey of quail, some of them chicks, darted out from the bushes and followed the first. They skittered across the road and disappeared into the brush on the other side. Then they flushed from the brush in an explosion of flapping wings.

Suddenly, a large military truck came careening around the bend. Bucky and Greg stopped in the middle of the road and stared with wide eyes as the truck barreled toward them. The driver blasted his horn and slammed on the brakes. The big truck skidded toward them in a crush of gravel and dust.

"Run!" Bucky yelled.

The two sheep bolted across the road. They leaped into a ditch as the truck skidded past, narrowly missing them.

The sheep crashed through the brush, leaping and bounding through the chaparral.

They stopped, both breathing heavily.

"Would you be more careful?" Greg asked.

"I was being careful."

They walked through the brush and out into a grassy clearing that sloped down to a gully. Chaparral grew in dispersed clumps throughout the clearing.

"I'm just saying you should be a little more careful. That truck almost killed us. It's been one near-death experience after the other. I want both of us to be a lot more careful from here on out. That means paying more attention to our surroundings."

"How was I supposed to know a truck was going to..."

The two sheep walked into a line of five soldiers who were standing at the edge of the clearing. The soldiers had their backs to the sheep.

They were shaving and brushing their teeth, splashing water from their canteens onto their faces, rinsing out their mouths and spitting onto the ground. Two were shirtless in the chill morning air.

"I've never seen anything like it. Two sheep running across the range under mortar fire."

"Will you stop talking about the sheep?" a big shirtless sergeant said. The big sergeant's face was slathered in shaving cream. He held a small mirror in his hand as he shaved with his razor.

"Velasquez was aiming for them. He nearly hit one."

"If he can't hit a sheep, how's he supposed to hit the enemy?"

"It wasn't only sheep down there. I swear I saw a kit fox."

"If I told you once I told you a million times. There was no kit fox."

"I'm not lying, sarge. I saw it running across the range."

"Kit foxes are an urban legend."

"This is the least urban place I've ever been."

"Maybe they're a rural legend."

"The two sheep went running in one direction and the kit fox in the other. It was the craziest thing I've ever seen."

"There was no kit fox."

"I know what I saw, sarge. It was a kit fox."

"It was probably a coyote."

"I've seen plenty of coyotes in my day and I know what I saw. It was definitely a kit fox."

"Don't go around telling anyone you saw a kit fox. We came down here to shoot mortars. If word gets out there's a kit fox on the range, that'll be the end of our training. Understand?"

"Then we can go home."

"No, you'll be back in garrison scrubbing toilets for the rest of the week. Make your choice."

"I don't know, sarge. Do you want us to be the unit that killed the last kit fox?"

"Enough about sheep and kit foxes. Personal hygiene is over. I want all of you in the truck in five mikes. Copy?"

"Yes, sergeant."

The big sergeant looked into his mirror as he shaved, angling it left and right.

"What the...?"

He turned around.

Bucky and Greg were slowly backing into the brush just a few feet from him.

"The sheep!"

The soldiers all turned around to see Bucky and Greg frozen in place looking up at them.

"Grab them."

The sergeant lunged forward. The two sheep darted from him and leaped into the chaparral. They ran through a line of parked military trucks and bounded right into a collection of camouflaged, one-man tents. Soldiers were emerging from the tents, putting on their boots or milling around. The two sheep ran between the tents. The big shirtless sergeant with shaving cream smeared across his face chased after the sheep between the tents.

"Don't let them get away!"

The sergeant tackled Greg to the ground. Greg struggled and kicked desperately as the shirtless sergeant wrestled him.

Greg baaed and bleated and kicked his legs. Soldiers peered over or around the tents watching the big sergeant wrestle with the sheep.

The soldiers from the clearing ran up behind him.

"Give me a hand, Thompson. Help me hold him down."

"I'm not a farmer, sergeant. I'm from Irvine."

The big sergeant pinned Greg to the ground with his elbows, pressing hard against Greg's ribs. The sergeant braced himself, digging into the mud with his boots, his backside sticking straight up in the air as he straightened his legs.

Bucky scratched the ground with his hooves and charged. He ran past the tents and gawking soldiers. His head smashed hard into the sergeant's posterior, sending the big man tumbling head over heels over the muddy ground. Greg quickly jumped to his feet.

"Run!"

The two sheep ran between the tents as soldiers tried to grab them. The sheep leaped into the brush and ran as hard as they could up the hillside with a dozen soldiers chasing behind them.

Tule Elk

"I'm just saying we need to be more careful. I don't think my heart can take many more of these close calls. We're taking too many risks."

"You're right. I know. But I think the worst of it is over."

"There's no reason to think that. We haven't reached the mountains yet. Our biggest challenge is still ahead of us."

The two sheep trudged up a steep hill. The air was cold. The sun broke through the gray clouds in places.

Atop the hill was a lone, leafless oak. Several dozen crows sat silently on the naked branches. Their black feathers were iridescent in the afternoon light. The big black birds seemingly filled every branch. The leafless tree, crowded with crows, stood in stark contrast against the overcast sky.

Bucky and Greg crested the hill. A single crow broke the silence with a loud caw-caw-caw. The others joined in filling the countryside with a chorus of angry caws. The crows took to the air as one in a fluttering of flapping wings and a cacophony of caw-caw-caws. The black flock flapped over the green hills and soared high into the gray sky.

From their vantage point atop the hill, the sheep looked out at the coastal mountains that were outlined against the darkening clouds. They gazed for a long moment at the mountain ridgeline.

"Liberty Mountain," Greg said.

"We're almost there."

The rocky peak of Liberty Mountain jutted up from the line of mountains to the west. Pine trees on the mountain ridges were silhouetted against the gray sky.

"Come on. It's not far now."

Below them were rolling hills covered in green grass. Only a few oaks grew on the hills, mostly in the arroyos. The hills rolled gently upward until merging with rocky, chaparral-covered foothills that climbed sharply to the mountains.

They walked down the hill in the high grass and then back up again. The two sheep walked up and down the rolling hills through the afternoon.

The sun fell low in the western sky. The afternoon sunlight cast dark shadows off the hills and trees. Turkey buzzards circled lazily above them. The air was cold in the shadows. Puffs of mists shot from their nostrils as they trudged up the shadowed hillsides.

The two sheep descended a gully where oaks grew along a water-filled channel. They leaped over the channel and climbed up the steep incline of the next hill.

"Stop," Bucky said. "Don't move."

"What is it?"

"Did you hear that?"

"Hear what?"

"I hear hooves. Something big. Many of them."

Greg's ears swiveled this way and that.

"I don't hear anything."

They continued onward through the grass. Bucky was alert as they walked slowly up the hillside. Greg walked beside him. His eyes darted left and right.

Bucky stopped dead in his tracks looking up to the crest of the hill.

At the crest, outlined against the winter sky, stood a majestic tule elk. It was as big as a horse and had a huge rack of white antlers atop its head. It stood tall, with head erect, looking forward. Its dark-colored legs were long, its body muscular and covered in tan fur, white at the rump but thick and dark around its long, shaggy neck. Its most impressive feature was its mighty rack of antlers that branched forward and upward, extending into numerous points as sharp as knives.

The big bull elk turned its head and looked down at Bucky and Greg who stood motionless in the grass. The two sheep looked up in awe at the giant elk.

The big buck raised up and bounded forward. It galloped along the hillcrest. More elk appeared atop the hill. They turned and galloped behind the big buck. Most had no antlers. One had a rack but it did not match the impressive antlers of the big buck. Another had a single antler atop its head; its antlers being shed after the end of the rutting season.

Several elk ran swiftly around the side of the hill and galloped past Bucky and Greg. More came.

They kept coming, more than a hundred of them. The big animals ran swiftly through the grass, their hooves clomping and stamping down the grass and dirt.

The elk picked up their pace and stampeded over and around the hill, galloping after the big buck. The earth shook from their hooves. Bucky and Greg feared they would be trampled as the herd of elk rumbled around them.

They ran with the herd. They baaed as they ran with them, trying to keep up with the giant animals that thundered over the grass.

The elk galloped down the hill and swiftly slipped into an oak-covered arroyo, leaving the two sheep on the hillside behind them.

As quickly as the elk had appeared they were gone, disappearing into the trees and hills.

Bucky and Greg stopped running before they reached the arroyo. They looked down the hillside at the arroyo and the dense cluster of oaks that filled it.

"Do you see them?" Bucky asked.

"No. No sign of them."

"They were huge. And so many of them."

Greg stood gazing down at the trees. "Sheep with racks of enormous antlers. A giant herd of them. When they run the earth shakes."

"Sheep as big as horses."

"Except they aren't sheep."

"No. It can't be."

Bucky stood silently for a moment gazing down into the oaks.

"I don't care what that stupid squirrel said. I know Zeus is there."

"It's unlikely, Bucky. No one's heard of any wild sheep living in the mountains. Not the pigs or the rabbit or the fox or that stupid squirrel."

"Why do you talk that way? What purpose does it serve? We've come too far to turn around now."

"Let's face facts. Even if we reach the top of Liberty Mountain, in all likelihood, Zeus and his flock won't be there. If we make it up there and they're not there, I don't want you to take it too hard."

"That's what I'm talking about. That right there. I'm tired of your negative attitude."

"I'm just being realistic."

"I'm tired of your constant complaining. Nobody likes it. It's why nobody likes you."

"I'm sorry. But hope can only take us so far. At some point we have to let go of hope and start to accept reality."

"Things are hard enough already. What's the point of complaining all the time? And you know what? I'm tired of your slow pace. I'm tired of your aches and your pains, and your doubts and worrying about every little thing. All your moaning and groaning. It only make things harder than they already are."

"That hasn't been my intent."

"I know Zeus will be there. I haven't come this far for nothing. He has to be there. I can feel it in my bones."

Bucky looked toward the rocky foothills and the steep slope of the ridges and the jagged peak of Liberty Mountain. Darkness was swiftly descending over the landscape.

"The steepest part of the trek is still ahead of us. We've got a hard climb before we reach the top. I need Zeus to be there. I need to believe he'll be there. It's what keeps me going."

"Then continue to believe, Bucky."

"I need you to just shut up. Shut up and walk."

Greg stood silently looking at his friend who stared forward at the hills. Greg turned and stepped forward through the grass.

Bucky stood still, watching Greg walk toward the peak of Liberty Mountain ahead of him in the distance. The rocky mountaintop jutted up from the ridgeline. The sun was setting behind it, silhouetting the jagged peak against the fiery orange sky.

The Lion

Darkness fell quickly over the hills. Low clouds rolled down the mountains and blocked the starlight.

The two sheep bedded down on a slope where the grass met the chaparral. The air was cold but windless, which made the chill slightly more bearable than the night before.

Bucky and Greg lay apart in the darkness. Greg chewed his cud. His lower jaw moved from side to side. He looked at Bucky over the grass as he chewed, holding a steady gaze through the darkness.

After some time, Bucky could take it no longer. "What are you doing?" he asked.

"Ruminating."

Greg looked away. He continued chewing his cud. He belched.

After a little while, the sound of chewing stopped. Greg was soon asleep. He breathed slowly, deeply and methodically.

Bucky remained awake brooding over the events of the day. Greg's labored breathing annoyed him. If only a different sheep were with him, he thought. Maybe Billy or Lulu. Or Mama.

If it weren't for Greg, he would probably have reached Liberty Mountain by now. And the hardships he had endured perhaps would seem half as heavy.

Bucky was weary. His muscles ached. His hooves were sore. He debated in his mind whether he should turn back and rejoin flock. It was Greg who had planted the thought in his head to leave the flock and start this trek into the wilderness to find Zeus and his wild sheep in the mountains. If it weren't for Greg, he wouldn't be sitting here in the cold on this faraway slope with no shepherd to watch over him and no dog to protect him. He would be back within the safety of the flock. He would be back with his loving Mama.

In the darkness, his mind went back and forth between turning back and continuing on. Both options were unappealing and filled him with dread. Continuing on meant a steep climb into the unknown and uncertain danger. If he continued and reached the top of Liberty Mountain, it seemed unlikely that Zeus and his flock would be there. What then? He would be alone with Greg in the wild atop a mountain far from his flock with no protection from predators and nowhere else to go except a long and treacherous journey back. He would again have to face the dangers of the soldiers, the explosions on the range, wild pigs, the raging river and the coyotes.

If he turned back now, he would forgo a treacherous climb and would be returning to the flock and to his Mama. But it meant giving up hope in the chance that Zeus and his wild flock might actually exist. If he were to make it back to the flock, he would forever wonder if Zeus was really there.

The debate in his mind tortured him until a heavy weariness pulled him downward into sleep. He slipped into a deep and dreamless oblivion.

He was uncertain how much time had elapsed when the morning sun warmed the inside of his eyelids with a red glow. He opened his eyes to a sunlit scene of green grass that merged with the darker green of the chaparral-covered foothills. Tan boulders jutted up from the chaparral into the sunlight.

Greg was no longer sleeping next to him. The grass where he had slept was flattened and compressed, but Greg was no longer there.

Bucky stood and searched for his troublesome companion. He spotted him grazing quietly several yards away. Bucky watched him for a long moment. Greg had lost considerable weight. He looked haggard and old.

Bucky grazed in the morning sunlight until he was full. Then he walked up the hill to where the grass met the chaparral. He stepped into the chaparral and made his way up the steep incline, picking his way over rocks and around sharp branches and prickly leaves. The branches and leaves clung to his wool and scratched his skin.

He climbed upward over the rocky soil, leaping up onto boulders and scaling cliff faces. He stopped atop a boulder, rested, and looked behind him.

Greg was following, trying to keep up. The old ram plodded on through the dense brush, breathing heavily.

Everything about Greg annoyed him—Greg's slow pace, his tired eyes, his groans and complaints, his belches, his cynicism, his negativity, his inability to get along with others.

Bucky debated whether he should just ditch him and continue on at his own pace. He could move much faster that way.

If only he had listened to Mama, he never would've thrown his lot in with old Greg, the outcast of the flock. He wouldn't be here in the wild in danger, but back within the safety of the flock.

Bucky jumped from the boulder and climbed higher and higher up the rocky soil.

The dirt terrain became progressively steeper. Interspersed here and there in the chaparral were sycamores and Torrey pines. Scrub oaks, wild lilac and manzanita shrubs with smooth, red bark on twisting branches, grew thick on the steep incline. Bucky walked parallel to the mountain face, picking his way through the brush, switching back and forth, winding upward against the steepness of the slope.

He stopped on a boulder and looked down at old Greg plodding along slowly through the manzanita. Bucky waited impatiently as Greg climbed toward him.

The sun shone down brightly. A hawk soared along the pines and rocks. It screeched a haunting, "keeeeee-ar." The cry carried on the wind and echoed off the rocks.

The top of the ridge was visible a few hundred yards above him. A bank of clouds was held back by the ridge—which seemed a dam of rock holding back the fog-filled sky. The cloudbank clung to the top of the ridgeline like powdery snow.

The chaparral was now thin on the rocky ground. The terrain had become steep, nearly vertical, and the climbing became increasingly difficult. Greg had nearly caught up. Bucky jumped from the boulder and walked along a rocky ledge that dropped precipitously beneath his hooves. The ledge was bordered on his left by a cliff face. Massive boulders jutted out from the cliff and hung over the steep drop.

Bucky's hooves loosened rocks, which tumbled from the ledge and bounced and crashed down the steep cliff. To his right, he looked down on the foothills and the green rolling hills and oaks. He could see for miles and miles from this altitude, all the way to the river and beyond to the faraway horizon. He walked carefully on the ledge, stopping every now and then to take in the lofty view. It was a beautiful view of the green world below—the most beautiful vista he had seen. It was the farthest he had ever seen.

Bucky stopped and turned and saw Greg behind him. Greg walked slowly and carefully along the ledge. The old ram walked under an outcropping of boulders. His head was down and his eyes looked tired.

Bucky waited for him to catch up, watching the haggard old sheep pick his way along the cliff face.

Movement on the boulder directly above Greg caught Bucky's eye. An enormous cat was atop the boulder, crouched down looking intently at the old sheep below. It was a mountain lion stalking its prey.

"Greg!"

The big lion leaped from the boulder and hissed a terrifying, "Raaaaooor!"

With its large front paws outstretched and claws extended, the lion landed on Greg's back. It sunk its dagger-like teeth into Greg's shoulders.

Greg baaed and bleated in pain and terror as the big cat knocked him flat and pinned him down on the rocky ledge with powerful jaws and claws.

An electric jolt of panic shot through Bucky. Greg looked at him from the rocks with the fear of death in his eyes. The big cat released its jaws and then bit down again into Greg's neck while holding him down with his sharp claws.

Bucky stood on the ledge with knees trembling as he watched the mountain lion sink in its teeth. Bucky was filled with fear and wanted to flee and escape down the ledge, but he couldn't bring himself to leave his friend.

Bucky scratched the ground with his front hoof, lowered his head and charged. He charged harder than he ever had in his life, kicking up rocks that tumbled and crashed down the cliff. He raised up on his back legs and threw his head forward with all his might as he lunged at the big mountain lion.

The cat stood up, growled, and in a flash, swatted its paw with claws extended. The claws slashed across Bucky's ribs with such force that he felt his body had ripped open. Bucky spun around from the force of the blow and fell stunned on the ledge. His head hung over the ledge looking downward at the rocky slope below.

Zeus

His pain was sharp and acute. It was the most pain he had ever felt, as if his ribs had been shattered and his body torn open.

He heard Greg's bleats.

Bucky lifted his head from the ledge and struggled to his feet.

The lion was atop Greg. The big cat watched Bucky calmly. It panted through its bloody jaws and let out a low throaty growl. It watched him through calm yellow eyes without the slightest sense of urgency, but with the relaxed confidence of an apex predator.

The mountain lion seemed to be waiting for Bucky to make a decision, to either charge again or flee.

Bucky knew another swipe of the lion's paw would be the end of him. If he turned and ran, he would be vulnerable to an attack from behind. He was frozen with indecision. He couldn't bring himself to turn and run. He didn't want to leave his friend. His legs wobbled, his knees shook. His heart pounded. Blood surged and pulsed through his veins.

Bucky's life flashed before his eyes. He saw the shepherd and the dog and the flock and his Mama. He saw the hills and arroyos and oaks.

His eyes met Greg's. He saw his friend's life draining away.

There was movement on the ledge behind the big cat. A mighty ram stepped around a large boulder. The ram was gigantic with massive spiral horns. The big ram stood on the ledge beneath the outcropping of boulders. It stood silently, quietly watching Bucky and the lion.

The lion saw in Bucky's eyes that something was behind it. The big cat turned its head and looked over its shoulder.

The ram charged across the ledge. It lifted its head and front hooves and sprang forward at tremendous speed. The lion leaped up and opened its front paws with claws extended. It let out a mighty roar as the two animals crashed together. The ram threw its head forward. Its huge horns smashed square into the lion's chest. The ram jerked its horned head upward and tossed the lion into the air.

The big cat flipped through the air several times and plunged over the ledge.

The ram skidded to a stop as rocks crashed down the cliff side.

"Follow me," he bellowed.

The mighty ram turned and bounded on the ledge and then leaped straight up the cliff face.

Bucky ran to Greg whose eyes were wild in delirium. Greg's neck and shoulder were covered in ghastly wounds and bright red blood.

Bucky nudged at Greg and helped him to his feet.

"Run if you want to live," the ram bellowed.

The two sheep ran on the ledge fueled by adrenaline and fear. The adrenaline surged through their blood as they chased the big ram straight up the steep mountainside.

They leaped and jumped after him between boulders and pines as cascades of rocks crashed down behind them. They ran and leaped and scrambled until Greg could run no longer. He collapsed on the rocks on the cliff side.

Bucky turned and ran back to him, breathing heavily. He attempted to nudge Greg to his feet, but exhaustion overtook him and he dropped onto the rocks next to him. He lay on his side on the rocks heaving and panting.

A shadow fell over him. He looked up to see a ram's head and giant horns against the blue sky.

"Zeus?"

"I am Zeus. What is your name, my friend?"

"Bucky. My name is Bucky."

"And your friend?"

"His name is Greg."

"Did you come from the flock beyond the river?"

Bucky nodded. He looked up at the ram in awe.

Zeus was the biggest sheep Bucky had ever seen. His body rippled with muscles. His curled horns seemed as thick as oak branches.

"Is your shepherd's named Pedro? His dog, Stevie?"

Bucky nodded still breathing heavily and rapidly.

"You've come a long way."

"I'd lost hope that you'd be here. I started to believe you were only a myth. A legend."

Zeus smiled. "I've been called worse."

"I can't believe we found you."

"You're a brave sheep, Bucky. Not many of us have survived a run-in with Puma. But you must learn to be more cautious in your movements. We could see you coming for miles, and so could Puma. He prowls these foothills and ridges and keeps a sharp eye out for wayward sheep. Many of us have been taken by him. I was lucky that I caught him by surprise. But I fear I only hurt his pride. He'll be after us if he isn't already. We can't stay here long."

Bucky lay on his side still trying to catch his breath as his heart raced and pounded in his chest. When his breathing and heartbeat finally slowed, he struggled to his feet.

Zeus stood over Greg sniffing and licking the bloody wounds on his shoulders and neck.

"You're a strong one, Greg. Puma did a number on you, but you survived. I need you to fight through the pain and follow me up the mountain. Do you understand? On Liberty Mountain, we'll be safe and you can rest. Now catch your breath. We'll need to move fast. On your feet."

Zeus nudged Greg up onto his feet. Bucky used his head to help hold Greg stable. Blood ran down Greg's legs and dripped from his nose.

"Follow me. It's not far now."

The big ram moved carefully and deliberately up the steep mountainside. Bucky and Greg followed him higher and higher up the rocky mountain face.

Bucky winced in pain with each step, forcing himself to continue onward. The scratches on his side throbbed and burned. He looked back at Greg. The bites and gashes on Greg's shoulders and neck were horrific. Claw marks ran up and down his sides. Greg walked slowly but Bucky saw determination and grit in the old sheep's eyes. Greg was bloodied and wounded but he was not giving up. He stared forward and onward as he climbed through the pain.

They followed the big ram up onto the ridgeline. The edge of the cloudbank spilled over the ridge like water over the top of a dam. The sheep walked between boulders that jutted dramatically upward into the mist.

The big ram leaped onto a massive, rounded rock. The two sheep followed him and walked cautiously along the rock face. They came around it and jumped down onto a rock-strewn cliff where pines clung to the mountainside.

A dozen sheep stood on the boulders looking down at Zeus, Bucky and Greg. The sheep jumped from the boulders and surrounded them.

"Any sign of Puma?" Zeus asked.

"No, Father," a young ewe said. "We've all been watching for him but it doesn't appear he's followed you."

"Everyone. I want you to meet Bucky and Greg. They come to us from Rancher Dave's flock. Please tend to their wounds."

"You're injured, Father."

The young ewe nuzzled her father and examined the red claw marks that ran across his rib cage.

"It's nothing, Maria. Tend to our new friends."

The sheep examined Bucky and Greg and licked their wounds.

Greg was a bloody mess. Bucky looked at him with worried eyes. He walked up to him and gazed on him with concern.

"I'm sorry, Bucky. I should've never doubted you."

Greg looked at Zeus and the flock of wild sheep that surrounded them. He looked back at Bucky and smiled a gap-toothed smile.

"We did it, Bucky. We made it."

Maria

The fog rolled over the ridge and engulfed the backside of mountain. Darkness fell quickly. Zeus and his flock huddled together between the boulders where they were protected from the cold mountain wind.

Bucky stood within the flock. Standing with them in the dark, he felt the same sense of comfort and security as he had back in the corral. He felt a sense of kinship with these wild sheep here on Liberty Mountain. But these sheep were different from those in the corral. They seemed more aware of their surroundings. They watched out for each other. They slept in shifts, some remaining awake and alert while the others snoozed.

Bucky watched Zeus in the misty darkness. The big ram stood tall amongst his flock, his massive horns visible in the mist. Zeus was awake, watching over them.

Greg was not standing with them. He lay on his side under a rocky outcropping that formed a shallow cave under the rock. One of the older ewes stood over him, occasionally sniffing and licking his wounds.

Bucky couldn't sleep. He left the flock and walked into the cave.

"He's resting now," the old ewe said. Her name was Rosy. She was the matriarch of this wild flock. "He's been in great pain, but he's finally fallen asleep."

"I'll watch him now. Please, get some rest."

The old ewe smiled and left him and returned to her flock.

Bucky stood over Greg. He watched his old friend breathe deeply and methodically, and worried about the severity of his ghastly wounds.

Eventually, Bucky drifted into sleep.

The fog lifted during the night and the stars appeared. Bucky awakened just before twilight. The stars twinkled over the eastern horizon that glowed as the dawn approached.

Greg still slept soundly on his side. The sun broke over the horizon and slowly revealed a spectacular view of the green hills. Mist filled the arroyos and valleys. The hills were islands in the white vapor.

All was visible from up here. The sheep of Liberty Mountain had a bird's-eye view of all the land. No predators could approach without being seen.

The old ewe stepped into the cave.

"The flock is leaving to graze. Go with them, Bucky. You must be hungry. I'll stay here with your friend."

Bucky hesitated, but she pushed him along with her muzzle.

Bucky reluctantly left the cave. He caught sight of the flock descending the mountain and trotted to catch them. They moved swiftly and surefootedly down the rocky mountainside.

They walked between boulders and past pines that were bent and twisted by the wind. The steep slope flattened into a small plateau that extended outward before dropping vertically from the mountain.

A cascade of water showered down from the cliff into a rocky pool at one end of the plateau. Beyond the pool, the plateau was covered with lush grass. The sheep grazed in the morning sunshine and drank from the clear pool beneath the waterfall.

Bucky gulped down gallons of water and then grazed voraciously.

"You must have hollow legs," Maria said.

Bucky looked up at her while chewing a large mouthful of grass.

"What do you mean?"

"I've never seen a sheep drink and eat so much. All that water and grass could hardly fit in your stomach alone."

"I'm a sheep. I have four stomachs."

Maria smiled at him.

She looked different from the ewes he had known. She wasn't round and plump, but lean and muscular. Her eyes were keen and had intelligence behind them. That being said, he felt in her smile that she possessed the same gentle kindness he had known in the ewes back in his own flock. Her warm smile reminded him of Mama.

"Does it hurt?" she asked, pointing with her nose at the claw marks on his side.

"Not so much now."

"Your friend. I hope he'll be OK."

"Me, too."

Bucky and Maria grazed together on the plateau. She told him about the flock and how she was born here on the mountainside only last spring. She said this plateau was one of several pastures the sheep grazed on. Each pasture had its time and season.

She asked many questions about his flock.

"It must be nice to have a shepherd to watch over you and a dog to protect you. Here on the mountain, we have no such protection. We must always remain vigilant and alert. Every spring the eagles come and snatch one or two of the newborn lambs. Every year, Puma comes and takes one or two of us. We do our best to avoid him but he's crafty and relentless. But then, you know all about Puma. It's terrible what he does. He fills us with great fear. I wish we had a shepherd and a dog."

"No. You're better off without them. Here on Liberty Mountain you're free. There are no humans to come and take you away. They take many more of us than any eagle or mountain lion."

She smiled at him. "I suppose the grass is always greener on the other side of the fence."

"Where I'm from, the sheep say there's danger beyond the fence."

"They're wise to say that."

Bucky looked out through the morning light at the view of the distant hills.

"I'm happy to be here. I've never seen a more beautiful place."

"It must have been a dangerous journey. You're a brave sheep, Bucky, to travel all this way, just the two of you."

"Maybe I'm brave, or maybe crazy."

She smiled at him bashfully and returned to grazing.

They spent the rest of the day together on the plateau grazing, chewing their cud and resting in the grass. The sheep took turns standing atop the boulders on the edges of the plateau, watching the mountainside for danger.

As evening approached, they made their way off the plateau and climbed back up the rocky cliffs.

"Bucky, do you like the views you've seen up here on Liberty Mountain?"

"Is it that obvious?"

"You keep staring into the distance and I worry you're not paying attention to the trail and may slip and fall."

"Don't worry about me, Maria."

"Would you like to see my favorite view?"

"Would I?"

She smiled. "Follow me."

Maria quietly broke away from the flock as the sheep walked along a ledge. She winked at Bucky and nodded forward with her nose.

The two sheep climbed straight up a boulder-strewn cliff. They switched back and forth up the cliff face, jumping from boulder to rocky ledge.

Scraggly pines grew at impossible angles from the rocks. Maria climbed higher and higher past the pines and boulders with the surefootedness of a mountain goat.

Bucky tried to keep up with her, and at a few points as he leaped from outcropping to outcropping, he feared he might fall hundreds of feet onto the rocks below.

Finally, they reached the peak where giant boulders reached up into the blue sky.

Bucky followed Maria through a narrow path carved between vertical walls of rock. She came around a bend and stopped. Bucky walked up beside her and looked out into what felt like eternity.

"It's the most amazing view I've ever seen."

The mountain dropped steeply down to craggy foothills that stretched for several miles until they abruptly ended in steep cliffs where the ocean smashed against the rocks. Beyond the cliffs and rocks was the eternal Pacific. The expanse of blue ocean seemed to stretch forever until merging in the faraway distance with the blue horizon. The sun was low in the western sky. White clouds sailed lightly above the white-capped sea.

They stood next to each other gazing in silence into the distance. She was close to him. He leaned against her. She did not pull away.

The sun sank beneath the clouds and illuminated them from below in a glow of painted colors that transformed the glimmering sky from pink to orange to purple and red.

"It's awesome," he said.

"I think so, too."

"This is my first time seeing the ocean."

"I'll take you down there some day."

"Being here now has made this whole journey worthwhile. All the hardship and fear and pain. It was worth it."

"It's getting dark. We better head back."

Bucky hesitated. He didn't want to leave. But she nudged him along and he followed her back down the steep cliffs.

Heaven

"Where have you been?" the old ewe demanded. "I've been worried sick about you."

"Oh, Mother."

The sheep were huddled together between the boulders in the dimness of the late evening light. Zeus was not with them.

"How many times have I told you that the flock must stay together? There's danger on the mountain."

Bucky left the flock and walked to the outcropping. Clouds rolled in over the mountain and further darkened the night sky. A light drizzle began to fall. In the far distance over the eastern hills, lightning flashed silently against the clouds.

Zeus emerged from under the outcropping of boulders as Bucky approached.

"You've returned. I was about to go looking for you."

"We went up the mountain and watched the sunset."

"Maria's favorite place."

"It's now my favorite place, too."

"I took her there as a lamb. Ever since, she wanders off when no one's looking and returns. She loves to be atop the mountain at sunset. But it is not safe to wander off alone. The flock must stay together, Bucky, especially with Puma prowling the mountainside. Maria has a mind of her own and can be impetuous. I ask that you use your better judgement to temper her ideas and notions when she wants to drag you off on some wild goose chase or needless adventure. Be her voice of reason. Goodness knows she no longer listens to me."

"Yes, Zeus."

The big ram looked over his shoulder to the cave. "Greg's injuries are severe. He's resting now. I brought him some forage. Stay with him and ensure that he eats."

Zeus turned and walked back to the flock.

Bucky stepped beneath the boulders and saw his friend sleeping on the rocky ground.

Under the outcropping, they were dry and protected from the light drizzle that was dampening the rocks outside.

Greg opened his eyes, looked up at Bucky and smiled.

"How are you feeling?"

"My bones ache. My muscles are sore. I have a headache. And I'm a little gassy."

"You should eat."

Bucky nudged the grass that Zeus had brought, pushing it toward Greg's mouth.

"Not now. Later."

"I have so much to tell you, Greg."

"I'm all ears."

Bucky told Greg about the plateau and the waterfall. He told him about the clear water beneath the falls and the lush green grass on the plateau. He told him of the spectacular views. He recounted how he and Maria had snuck away from the flock and climbed up the steep cliffs.

Greg smiled. "You little devil. She's a looker."

Bucky told him how they had reached the mountaintop and walked between the boulders until the endless ocean unfolded to the horizon before them. He described the colors of the sunset and how the sun slowly sank into the sea.

"It's like heaven here. As soon as you're well, I'll take you up there, Greg. You're going to love it. And wait till you see the plateau. The grass there is the most delicious you've ever tasted. Way better than the pastures we're used to. I can't wait to show you."

"You already have."

He told him about Zeus, how big and powerful and wise he was, how he watched over the flock better than any shepherd or dog ever could.

Greg smiled. "He's magnificent."

"I have to admit, Greg, I was angry at you. I was starting to think you were just some crazy old sheep, that you'd made everything up and there was no Zeus and no wild flock. But now here we are on top of the world. Everything was true. And it's far better than I could've ever imagined. I'm happy that I listened to you instead of staying with the flock and following all those silly sheepisms for the rest of my life."

"We've had quite the adventure, haven't we?"

"Yes, we have. What's funny is the sheep here think we're some kind of heroes for coming all this way alone through the wilderness. Can you imagine? You and me, Greg. Heroes. Even Zeus is impressed by what we did."

"Thank you for bringing me here, Bucky."

"You've been right all along. I've been careless and reckless. From now on, I'm going to listen and I won't take any more needless risks. I'll think things through before I act. I'll pay attention. Like Zeus does. Here in the wild we have no shepherd to watch over us and no dog to protect us. But we have each other. We must rely on our senses and our strength and speed. We have to rely on each other. It's true there's danger beyond the fence, but there's freedom, too. No humans can come for us here to take us away. As long as we stick together and watch out for each other, we'll be safe here. I think we're going to have a great life here. We'll be happy here."

"I'm happy now."

Lightning flashed and danced across the clouds on the eastern horizon. The slow rumble of thunder reached them a moment later. The drizzle had stopped. They watched in the darkness as the lightning flashed and flickered across the clouds.

"It's heaven here," Greg said.

"Get some rest. I need you to get better and back on your feet. I have so much to show you."

Bucky stood under the rocks, silhouetted against the dark sky. The silent lightning flashed against the distant clouds and lit the cave in flickering light.

Greg closed his eyes.

"You've been a good friend," he said. "You've been my only friend."

Bucky looked out at the lightning as it danced across the night. It flashed and spread electric fingers over the distant clouds, like spider webs across the night sky.

"Did you see that one? That was the best yet."

Bucky watched the flashes of light for a long moment.

"The sheep here are different from those back in the flock. They pay attention to the Earth and the wind and all the creatures of the world. I suppose they need to with no shepherd and no dog to be their eyes and ears. They're not judgmental. They don't just follow along blindly, but think things through. They control their own destinies. We're going to fit in here, Greg. You're going to fit in here. This is the right place for us. It's the right place for you. You and me. We can do anything if we stick together."

Bucky looked down at his friend.

"Greg."

He leaned down and sniffed him and nudged him with his muzzle.

The air turned cold. The wind gusted.

"Greg?"

The tears welled up in Bucky's eyes. The drizzle turned to rain.

"Please, Greg. No."

The rain poured down in a deluge from the dark sky.

The Leader

Bucky didn't leave the cave for two days. A dark depression had seized hold of him. He stayed unmoving in the cave, not leaving Greg's side, not eating, but staring with blank eyes into the eastern sky.

The sheep had tried to coax him out but he ignored them. Zeus had come and tried to talk him out to no avail.

The sadness had paralyzed him. He longed to be back with his Mama.

Another night passed and the dawn came. Rosy stepped into the cave.

"You must eat."

She nudged him with her muzzle. In his hunger and thirst he was too weak to resist. The old ewe pushed him out from under the rocky overhang.

It was a misty morning. Old Rosy walked behind him and pushed him along as the flock descended the steep mountain face. They reached the plateau.

She pushed him to the pool of water. His thirst took hold and he drank from the pool by the gallon.

Bucky stood staring blankly at his reflection in the pool. His eyes were red and tired. He felt old and worn out.

"Please eat," Maria said.

She nuzzled up against him and tried to nudge him toward the grass. He pulled away from her and walked out onto the plateau away from the other sheep.

"Bucky, please. It's terrible seeing you like this. Come talk to me."

He walked away from her to the edge of the plateau and stood on the ledge looking down at the world beneath him.

Zeus approached and stood next to him on the ledge.

"Greg was my son," the big ram said. "I hadn't realized it, but when you were gone I went to him and we spoke and he told me about the night when we fled the corral. Nearly a hundred sheep from the flock followed me out of the corral that night. Greg was one of them. We ran through the hills as the dog and the shepherd chased after us. Greg was one of the first chased down by the dog. The shepherd and the dog captured and rounded up many of us before we reached the river. Some of us escaped them and reached the water's edge. Some turned back too afraid to cross. The rest of us splashed across the river. It was shallow and easy to cross. It had been a dry winter that year not nearly as wet and stormy as this one. We made it to the other side and the coyotes came after us. They took several of us. They hounded us and harassed us as we fled through the hills. Some of the sheep collapsed and died from exhaustion on our flight. We reached the foothills and began our climb upward. Puma was waiting for us in the chaparral. He took one of my older sons. By the time we reached the peak of Liberty Mountain, only twenty of us were left. Twenty out of a hundred. The hardship of life here in the wild took more of us. The cold, the hunger, the fear. We were domesticated animals trying to survive without the help of human hands. It was a difficult time for us. I questioned myself and what I had done—what I had subjected my followers to. For some strange reason, they believed in me. They stayed with me and we struggled through the cold and the wind and the hunger. We made it through that first winter and into spring. Some of the ewes birthed lambs. We learned the ways of the wild and made a life for ourselves here. But every year some of us are lost—to Puma, to eagles, to illness. I'm older now. My teeth are gone and it's hard for me to eat. I'm still big and strong, but a little less so each passing season. I'm not long for this world. We need new blood here. New youth and vigor. New leadership."

Zeus looked at Bucky who stared into the far-off distance.

"All these years I thought Greg had been taken back to the flock and had long ago been butchered and eaten by the humans. I'm happy to know he lived a long life and that he finally managed to escape. I know it's hard to lose your friend. I've lost another son. But as leaders we must remain strong, or at least appear so, even though the pain and sorrow are tearing us apart inside."

"He would still be alive if we had stayed with our flock."

Zeus looked out into the distance. "He told me this is what he always wanted—to escape the flock and come here and find us. He told me he wouldn't have had it any other way."

"I should've never made him come here. He'd still be alive if it weren't for me."

"Don't blame yourself for his death. He didn't blame you."

"I said cruel things to him the day we reached the foothills. I regret that I ever said them. I didn't apologize to him for what I said."

They stood silently on the ledge looking out into the distance.

"I see something in you, Bucky. Something in the way you carry yourself, in your eyes and in your voice. You see farther than other sheep. You understand things that they are unable to know. We sheep are social animals. We're not solitary, like Puma, but need each other to survive. Sheep are born followers. Only a few are born to lead. Everyone can see when they look at you that you are a born leader. They want to follow you."

"That's what they told me back at my flock. But no one ever asked me if that was what I wanted."

Zeus smiled. "Oftentimes the best leader is he who doesn't seek it. Every sheep must find his place in the flock, Bucky. That is our way. You must find your place, your purpose. And when you find it, you must embrace it with all your being."

"I want Greg back. I'd give anything to have him back again."

"You're in mourning. That is natural and understandable. You and Greg were close. I want you to stay close to me. I will teach you the ways of the wild. I will teach you how to lead the flock. I will teach you our sheepisms."

The Tag

Zeus repeated the sheepisms of his wild flock. Many were the same sheepisms from Rancher Dave's flock, but some were new and unfamiliar.

"The flock must stay together. A sheep alone is a sheep in danger. Puma prowls at night. He pounces from the treetops and boulders."

"I hated the sheepisms when I was back with my flock," Bucky said, "the way sheep mindlessly repeated them. It was one of the reasons I wanted to escape and come here."

"I was contemptuous of them, too. Sheepisms made me think that sheep had no thoughts of their own—that they were incapable of original thinking and only repeated what came down to them. Back then, I saw through the purpose of the sheepisms. They were meant to keep the flock together and full of fear so we wouldn't run away. The sheepisms didn't serve our interests, but instead the interests of Rancher Dave who kept us for the slaughter. I vowed to escape and found a new flock of free thinking sheep, without sheepisms to dull our minds. But here on the mountain, I saw the need for new sheepisms. Most sheep are not like you and Greg. They are not free thinkers, especially the young, the inexperienced and the slow of mind. Most sheep don't think. They know not from experience and observation, but only what is repeated in the flock. Sheepisms organize their thoughts and behaviors. Few sheep will seek the truth and follow it wherever it may lead. As long as they feel safe, their bellies are full and they are accepted by the flock, they're content. They'll accept and repeat any old sheepism that comes down to them, even a false one, if it serves the status quo. They'll react angrily to any truth that challenges their established beliefs, and they'll turn on you. It took me some time to come to terms with this observation. But once I did, I set about devising new sheepisms that did not serve the interests of Rancher Dave and the humans, but instead the interests of our flock here on the mountain. I saw that sheepisms can have value. The right sheepism can protect a sheep and empower him. It can guide him down the correct path. I devised sheepisms that guided our behavior, to keep us safe from danger, to keep us healthy and well-fed. These sheepisms are our hard-won knowledge that help us survive. You, Bucky, are bright enough to look at the world and understand what you see. You can think for yourself. This at times may seem a great burden and a frustration when others are unable to see and understand the world like you do, but are only capable of repeating sheepisms planted in their heads by others. But being bright is a gift of nature.

For you, sheepisms are not a substitute for thinking, but a tool you can use to guide the thoughts and behaviors of others."

"It's strange to think this way."

"When you are a leader, you are required to use your mind. You can use it for good or ill. Those leaders that are dull-minded and selfish will not be loved. They are despised. But those who put the interests of the flock first will be revered. I have made many mistakes as a leader, but I always wanted the best for the flock, for each and every sheep. Sheep can sense this. They sensed that I had their best interests at heart and they forgave my mistakes. I grew as a leader and learned and became wiser. You will learn and grow, too. Just remember to strive to do right by them. Earn their trust through your actions. Whether they understand your intentions or not, they will sense them, and they will follow you to the ends of the Earth if you ask them."

"How did you learn that the humans keep us for food?"

"That was a secret that was revealed to me inadvertently, but once I learned the truth, it changed the course of my life and the lives of those who believed in me. Back when I was the leader of Rancher Dave's flock, the dog and I had become close friends. Stevie was young and inexperienced then. He was still learning how to protect us from predators and how to keep the flock together. He looked up to me as an experienced leader, watched me and listened to me. We would sit in the grass together and he would listen to my stories. I would ask him questions and he would answer without thinking through the implications of what he told me. It was through our conversations that I learned that the humans take away our lambs every summer, not to greener pastures, but to a slaughterhouse to butcher them for meat. Stevie told me this not thinking much of it. To him it was just the way of things. We all had our place. The human place was at the top, the dogs under them and we sheep were further down the ladder. He thought in my wisdom that I knew this and accepted it as the natural order of the world. I learned from him that in the winter, around this time of year, Rancher Dave selects animals from each of his herds and flocks. A sheep, a cow, a pig. The chickens and ducks, too. Stevie told me that Rancher Dave decorates his house with lights and the humans come from all around for a giant feast. Roast beef, ham, grilled mutton, chicken and duck. The humans gorge themselves on the flesh of his animals. I remember vividly that winter long ago when Rancher Dave came to the flock and selected Rosy for the feast. Before he could take her away, I decided to make our escape. I spoke to the flock telling them all I had learned. But I spoke a little too wildly and was loose with my emotions. I told them that everything they'd ever known was a lie. My words were too much for most of them to believe. I revealed too much too soon. They thought I had lost my mind. I could see it in their eyes. This angered me. I was angered by their stupidity and their inability to accept the truth. I insulted those who wouldn't believe me. My mistake was that I let my emotions show. They saw my fear and anger and my contempt and they lost faith in my leadership. Sheep will follow a steadfast and strong leader, but they become nervous and frightened when they sense fear and anger. I told them that their whole world was a lie and demanded that they follow me out into the unknown, into the dangers of the wild. In hindsight, I see the mistakes I made. I would have approached them differently if I knew then what I know now about leading sheep."

Rosy walked up behind them and joined them on the ledge. She ran her muzzle under Zeus's neck. He smiled and returned her affection.

"You saved Rosy."

"Yes, he saved me," Rosy said. "He saved all of us here."

"How did you know Rancher Dave was going to take her?"

"Stevie told me that every winter Rancher Dave clips a yellow tag to the ear of the sheep he has selected for the feast. When I saw the yellow tag on Rosy's ear, I had to act. I couldn't let him take her. I wouldn't have been able to live with myself."

Rosy tilted her head and showed Bucky her ear.

Clipped on her ear was a dirty piece of plastic. Bucky examined it closely. It was worn and cracked at the edges and the yellow color had long faded, but Bucky had seen this type of tag before.

He had seen the same tag clipped to Mama's ear.

"Bucky?" Rosy asked. "What's wrong?"

Bucky stepped back from the ledge. His eyes had a hollow distant look. He walked backward through the grass away from them.

Run

"Mama."

"Bucky?" Rosy asked with concern.

Bucky turned and trotted along the ledge. He leaped down the cliff face jumping recklessly from boulder to ledge.

"Come back, Bucky," Zeus bellowed.

Bucky leaped and jumped down the cliff face. Rocks rolled and crashed in front of him as he scrambled downward. He eventually reached the bottom of the steep cliff and leaped over rocks and through the brush. He made his way down the rugged foothills running swiftly through the manzanita and around the boulders and pines. The thorny branches and prickly leaves of the chaparral caught on his wool and scratched his skin. He ran out from the chaparral onto the green grass of the rolling hills. He ran up and down the hills and through the arroyos, tracing the route he had taken with Greg only a few days before. He continued running through the afternoon until darkness fell.

He ran through the night until he reached the range. Without hesitating he ran across it, running around craters and past the shattered hulk of the tank, fully expecting the dark earth to erupt under his feet. His muscles were weak and his lungs burned when he reached the edge of the range, but he continued running.

The sun was rising in the east under a thick cover of clouds. He reached the oak forest. He ran through the trees and over the torn-up ground until he reached the swollen river. He did not stop but leaped from the bank into the roiling water. He kicked hard with all four legs as the current spun him around and around and swept him downstream. He was far down the river when he washed up on the rocks on the opposite bank. He dragged himself out of the water and scrambled up the muddy bank. He ran over the gravel road and across the grassy plain.

The sky was dark and overcast. As he ran, he saw movement to his right. Two coyotes ran down a hillside toward him. Fear pulsed through him. He ran up the hill in front of him and dashed through the oaks. He ran down the opposite side of the hill looking over his shoulder for the coyotes.

The coyotes ran swiftly through the oaks, gaining on him.

Bucky turned and ran through a narrow arroyo. The coyotes were on his heels. He heard their snarls as he ran. One sank its sharp teeth into his rump. He kicked with his back legs and struck the coyote in the throat. The other coyote nipped his flank. He couldn't keep running like this allowing them to bite and tear at him from behind.

He skidded to a stop and spun around and faced them. The coyotes stood in front of him, pacing back and forth, heads down, their long, bushy tails swishing as they turned. They watched him with hungry eyes.

One of them leaped forward with fangs bared. Bucky raised up and stomped at the coyote with his front hooves. He connected with a hoof that struck the coyote between its eyes. Bucky rapidly stomped again and again fueled by rage and fear. The coyote yelped in pain and backed off.

The second coyote lunged for Bucky's throat. Bucky raised up and stomped the coyote in the back of the neck. He stomped with great fury again and again. The second coyote yelped in pain and backed away.

The two canines paced back and forth in front of him growling until finally lunging together for his throat. Bucky stomped with all his might, landing blow after blow at the startled coyotes. He lowered his head and charged, catching one of the coyotes in the ribs. He jerked his head upward and tossed the coyote into the air. It flipped round and round and landed on its back on the rocks. It jumped to its feet and ran away yelping with its tail between its legs.

Bucky charged the second coyote which retreated after its friend.

Bucky turned and ran through the arroyo and up into the hills. It was late afternoon when he reached the eucalyptus grove. He plunged into the grove beneath the towering trees and emerged on the other side. He bounded through the high grass until he finally reached the barbed wire fence.

As he ran along the fence, exhaustion set in. His muscles ached, his hooves were sore, his lungs were burning, his vision was blurry. But he continued onward, running along the fence. In the twilight, he saw ahead of him a gnarled and twisted oak atop an outcropping of boulders. He ran around the oak and up the hillside.

Atop the hill he saw the truck and camper and the shepherd shack. He stopped and hid behind the oaks and slowly approached the corral looking for signs of the shepherd and the dog.

The shepherd opened the gate to the corral. Papa ran inside. The sheep followed him baaing as they ran to the trough. Stevie barked at the stragglers and herded them into the corral.

Pedro shut the gate and counted the sheep. Bucky laid low. He made his way through the trees to the opposite side of the corral.

Pedro eventually left the corral and walked under the trees to the shepherd shack. He entered the door and Stevie followed him. The old shepherd shut the door behind him.

Bucky crept up to the fence and looked through the wooden slats. The sheep were mulling around in the dark, preparing to sleep. Bucky caught sight of Lulu and made his way along the slats toward her.

"Lulu."

Bucky called to her several times until he finally got her attention.

"Lulu. Come here."

She walked up to the slats curiously.

"It's me. Bucky."

"Oh, my goodness, Bucky. You're alive."

"Where's Mama?"

"Mama?"

"Where's my Mama?"

"Rancher Dave came this morning and took her away to greener pastures."

Bucky backed away from the slats. He turned and ran from the corral.

"Bucky!"

He ran down the hill and back to the twisted oak tree. He ran up the sloping incline and leaped over the barbed wire fence. He landed at a run and galloped in the dark along the vineyards and down the gravel road. He ran and ran until the fence turned ninety degrees to the south. Bucky turned and ran along it past endless vineyards and through the cow pastures, following the fence up and down the hills and through the trees.

He ran and ran. He lost feeling in his legs. His lungs burned. His eyes played tricks on him in the dark. He wheezed as he ran.

As he ran up a steep slope, his legs gave out. He tripped and fell and slid down the slope.

He lay in the mud at the bottom of the steep slope. He was unsure how long he had been unconscious. A bolt of fear shot through him. He worried that he may be too late, that Rachel and her family might have already eaten Mama. He pulled himself onto his feet, his legs trembling, his lungs aching. He dragged himself, step by step, exhausted, up and down the hills, until night turned to dawn.

The sun broke the edge of the eastern horizon. In the distance, he saw a ranch house strung with lights on a hill. He saw the red barn where he had been nursed back to health.

He dragged his numb body across the pastures toward the barn. Mist rose from the frosty grass. Roosters crowed.

Bucky froze when he heard the barking of dogs. He hid behind a broken-down truck overgrown with grass. The grass grew high around its baseboard and fenders. Bucky stood behind the truck and listened. He couldn't see straight. His legs were weak. The world faded in and out of focus.

He heard the baas of a sheep. He could recognize those baas anywhere. It was his Mama and she was crying out in fear.

The Butcher

Rancher Dave and Rachel led Mama by a halter from the barn and down a gravel road that led to a cinderblock structure. The structure had a metal roof and a large metal roll-up door that was pulled open.

The sky was dark and overcast this chilly morning. A few raindrops fell here and there in the whispering breeze.

Rancher Dave and Rachel led Mama through the metal doorway to where a butcher stood waiting on the cement floor. The butcher was a big man with a bushy blonde beard. He wore a butcher's frock that was smeared with blood. The carcasses of a cow and a pig hung from meat hooks attached to chains wrapped around the metal rafters. Blood from the carcasses dripped and flowed to a drain in the cement floor.

"One more to go, Jerry," Rancher Dave said.

"She's a beauty," the butcher said, eyeing Mama.

Tiger walked atop the railing of one of the cement stalls that lined the walls of the slaughterhouse. The striped cat sat at the end of the railing and swished his tail as he watched Mama.

Rancher Dave and Rachel led Mama to the butcher.

"She's calm now," Rancher Dave said. "We don't need to tie her down."

The butcher walked over to the corner of the room where he kept his tools on a wooden table. On the table were meat hooks, a long knife and a butcher's saw. The butcher picked up a shotgun that was leaned in the corner.

Rancher Dave led Mama back out the doorway and stopped in the gravel just outside the slaughterhouse door. He placed a pan of feed in front of Mama who sniffed it and then nibbled on the hay. He set down the halter rope and stepped back.

Rachel kneeled down in front of Mama who looked up at her. Mama chewed on the hay as she looked at the little girl's face. Rachel held Mama's face in her hands.

"I'm sorry we have to do this to you. You've been a good sheepy."

"Come here, Rachel," Rancher Dave said.

The butcher walked out the large doorway holding the shotgun at his side. He walked up to Mama.

"Step back. Cover your ears."

He raised the muzzle and aimed it at the middle of her forehead above her eyes.

Rachel hugged her father and looked away. Rancher Dave cupped his hand over his daughter's exposed ear. As she pressed her face against her father's jacket, she saw Bucky standing in the grass under the gray sky, the red barn behind him.

"Daddy, look."

Bucky bleated.

Mama turned her head and saw him. She baaed to him. She took a step forward.

The butcher leaned down and grabbed the halter. Mama baaed as the butcher pulled her back into position.

Bucky was worn out and exhausted. His fleece was covered in red scratches and caked with mud. His legs were shaking. He baaed, lowered his head, scratched the ground with his front hoof and charged across the grass.

The butcher released Mama, set down his shotgun and stood up. He stepped backward onto the cement floor of the slaughterhouse as Bucky charged into him. The butcher leaned down, grabbed Bucky by the legs and flipped him onto his side. Bucky baaed and struggled as the butcher pinned him to the floor. Rancher Dave ran over and helped the butcher hold him down.

"Get him into the stall," Rancher Dave said.

The two men shoved Bucky across the cement floor and into a stall. The butcher shut the iron gate with a clang.

Bucky baaed for his mother. Mama trotted over to him and pressed her nose through the iron gate. The two sheep touched noses and bleated.

"Are we butchering two sheep this year?" the butcher asked.

"I don't know where that one came from," Rancher Dave said.

"Daddy, that's the little sheepy that was attacked by the coyotes."

"The one you tended in the barn?"

"Yes. He must've come for his mommy."

The butcher grabbed the halter and pulled Mama back to the doorway. She resisted and baaed for her son.

Tiger sat up on the railing swishing his tail, watching the proceedings with keen interest.

"Have you ever seen anything like it?" the butcher asked as he pulled Mama. "It's the darndest thing I've ever seen."

"Daddy, he came back to save his mommy from the butcher."

"Are you telling me a sheep came all this way from the flock to save his mother?"

"Yes, Daddy. Can't you tell? Look at him. He loves his mommy."

"Let's take him to the barn. Jerry's got work to do."

Rancher Dave grabbed another halter from a hook on the wall and walked over to the stall. He opened the gate and grabbed Bucky by the wool. Bucky struggled and baaed as Rancher Dave tried to place the halter on him.

"He doesn't want to leave his mommy. He doesn't want us to kill her. Please, Daddy. Can't you see? The little sheepy loves her."

"Rachel, you're anthropomorphizing the animals."

"I'm what the animals?"

Rancher Dave stepped back and closed the gate. He kneeled down and took his daughter's hand.

"Honey, someday this ranch will be yours. I know you like tending to the sheep and the chickens and you've grown attached to them. But we make our livelihood from the land and from the animals. They provide us with income and sustenance. In our line of work, we can't become emotionally attached to the livestock."

"Please, Daddy. Can we not serve mutton this year?"

"Now, you know, honey, it's our family tradition. We take one of the animals from each of our flocks and herds and serve them at our holiday meal. It's our way of expressing our gratitude for all the Lord's blessings he's bestowed on us. It's how we give thanks for our good fortune."

"Oh, Daddy. No one touched the mutton last year."

"We all love your mother's mutton recipe—garlic peppered with crushed rosemary, and her redcurrant jelly."

"You're the only one who likes it, Dad."

"Come, Rachel. Jerry's waiting."

The little girl hugged her father and held him tight.

"Please, Daddy. Let the little sheepy be with his mommy. Please? It's Christmas."

Rancher Dave stood up and shook his head.

"I think we'll skip the mutton this year, Jerry."

The butcher stood holding Mama by the halter with the shotgun at his side.

"Good call, Dave."

Tiger leaped down from the railing and walked across the cement floor. The cat looked over its shoulder, swished its tail and walked out the door with nose held haughtily in the air.

Bucky baaed for Mama and she baaed back. The butcher shook his head and turned and opened the gate.

Bucky ran out to his mother and nuzzled his nose against hers.

"I've never seen anything like it," the butcher said. "He sure loves his mama."

Molasses

The soft coos of doves carried through the rafters. Bucky lay on his side in the straw. He felt his mother's gentle presence. A warm peaceful feeling washed over him. He was unsure how long he had been unconscious but felt it must have been quite some time.

Rachel had led him and Mama out of the slaughterhouse under a gray sky. Bucky could barely walk. His knees were wobbly and his legs weak. His vision was blurry as he staggered to the barn behind Rachel and Mama. He had collapsed with exhaustion in the stall.

He felt his mother's warm muzzle on his face and neck.

"You need to eat."

He opened his eyes and saw her standing over him looking at him with motherly concern and affection. His eyes watered up upon seeing her face. He had missed her so much.

She helped him onto his feet and over to the water trough. He lapped up the cold water. The food trough was filled with alfalfa, carrots, rutabagas, turnips and beets. He was famished and ate until his belly ached. The feed here tasted even better than he remembered.

"Oh, Bucky."

"It's good to see you, Mama."

"You strayed from the flock and I was certain you'd been eaten. Then, at my darkest moment, you appeared. It was a miracle." She smiled at him. "I missed you terribly."

"I missed you, too."

Bucky and Mama relaxed in the stall talking happily, enjoying each other's company. Bucky told her of his adventures. Mama listened with great interest, worry and fear. He told her of all the animals they had met. He told her of the predators. The dangers beyond the fence were worse than she had imagined.

He told her how they had finally reached Liberty Mountain and had been attacked by Puma but were saved by Zeus. He told her of the magnificent Zeus and his wild flock.

"Yes, I remember him from when I was lamb. I remember him every bit as magnificent as you say."

He told her about Rosy and Maria and the sunset over the ocean. His eyes filled with tears as he recounted the demise of Greg. He told her how Zeus had told him the meaning of the yellow tag and how he had run through the wilderness to find her.

"Oh, Bucky. Why did you ever leave me? You knew there was danger beyond the fence. But you've always been headstrong and reckless. You never listen to your poor, suffering Mama."

Rachel entered the barn and approached the stall.

"Hello, sheepies."

She opened the gate and kneeled in the straw. She held a glass jar of molasses. She dipped a wooden spoon into it and held the spoon out to them. Mama eagerly approached her and licked the molasses from the spoon.

She baaed for Bucky but he refused to approach Rachel. He stood at the back of the stall looking away from her.

"Come here, sheepy," Rachel said, holding out the spoon. "What's wrong? I know you love molasses."

But Bucky stayed away.

"Rachel, it's time for school."

"Coming, Daddy."

She got up and left the barn taking her jar and spoon.

"How can you go to her after all we know?"

"She's just a little girl, Bucky. She wants us to be happy, and nothing makes a sheep happier than molasses."

Bucky and Mama remained in the stall for several days. The mare and her foal were no longer around and Tiger stayed away. Their only company were the doves and Rachel who came to them every morning. Bucky resisted going to her but the temptation of the molasses became too great and he finally gave in.

"It's delicious. Isn't it, little sheepy? I knew you love molasses."

One morning as they ate from the trough, the mice appeared. Bucky dropped a turnip for them.

"Thank you, Mr. Sheep. It's good to see you again."

"It's good to see you, too."

Tiger sauntered in through the barn's front door.

"The cat is coming," Bucky said. "Run and hide."

The three little mice scurried away into the hay.

Tiger walked up to the gate and looked at the sheep. He sashayed back and forth along the slats.

"It's too bad Rachel has such sway over her father. I was looking forward to mutton this year."

"Go away, Tiger."

The cat sat and watched them through the slats. He sniffed the air. "The mice have been in your stall. Where did they go?"

"Shhh," Bucky said. "Do you want to know where they went?" he whispered.

Tiger smiled and nodded his head.

Bucky walked up to the slats. Tiger's tail swished back and forth on the hay. It swished under the gate.

Bucky leaned down and Tiger leaned forward smiling. Bucky stomped a front hoof hard onto Tiger's tail. The cat let out a yowl and bolted across the barn floor and out the door.

"Goodness, Bucky. Why did you do that to that poor cat?"

"He had it coming."

In the afternoon, Rancher Dave pulled up to the barn in his truck in a crunch of gravel. He led Bucky and Mama out of the stall and into the trailer. He slammed the trailer gate shut and started up the truck's engine.

They bounced down the road past the vineyards and the horse and cow pastures. They drove out onto the highway through the green countryside until they reached a military gate. The soldier at the guard shack walked around the trailer and looked in at the sheep. He waved Rancher Dave through the gate. The truck bounced along the road past row after row of army barracks. Rancher Dave drove away from the cantonment area and into rolling hills scattered with oaks. He turned off the paved road and onto a muddy track that led up to a ridgeline. The truck and trailer bounced along the ridge until finally coming to a stop next to the shepherd shack. Rancher Dave walked around to the back of the trailer, lowered the gate and pulled the two sheep out by their wool.

From atop the hill, Bucky and Mama could see the flock grazing below under the sun in a field of green grass. Mama baaed to them. The sheep looked up and baaed back.

"Come, Bucky," Mama said with great happiness. "Let's return to the fold."

She turned and trotted down the hill. He had never seen Mama run with such energy. They entered the flock together and all the sheep gathered around.

"It's Mama."

"And Bucky."

"They're alive."

"It's so good to see you."

"Where have you been?"

"Were the pastures really greener?"

"We thought you'd been eaten."

"It's a miracle."

All the ewes looked at Bucky with great interest and admiration. Bucky spotted Lulu among them. She was obviously happy to see him again. He walked up to her.

"Oh, Bucky. I've been so worried about you. I never thought I'd see you again. Then you appeared in the night and I thought it was a dream. Now you're back. It's wonderful to see you."

"It's good to see you, too, Lulu."

The two young sheep rubbed their noses together. Bucky truly was happy to see her. He wished he'd never left.

"Oh, Bucky."

Papa stood tall in the flock looking down at them. His eyes locked onto Bucky's and narrowed.

"I need to have a word with you," Papa said with authority.

The ewes fell silent. They looked up at Papa with great worry, sensing anger in the tone of his voice. It was the tone he used right before he gave some hapless sheep a thrashing.

"Come here, Bucky. Now."

Papa

The ewes parted as Papa walked between them. He stopped and looked down his nose at Bucky.

"Do you think you can spread fear and dissension in my flock and run off only to return as if nothing has happened?"

"I never meant to spread fear or dissension or to upset you, Papa."

"It matters not what you meant to do. What matters is what you've done."

Papa looked at Bucky with anger and contempt. But Bucky stood his ground and didn't lower his head deferentially like the other sheep. He met Papa's angry glare without looking away.

For the first time, Bucky noticed Papa's age. The old ram was missing some of his teeth. While still slightly larger than Bucky, Papa's build lacked the muscles and hardness forged through the trials and ordeals of the wild. Papa didn't compare to Zeus in size or stature. He was smaller and plumper and his eyes lacked Zeus's keen intelligence.

"I'm banishing you from the flock."

The ewes gasped.

Bucky stood before Papa watching the old ram posture in front of him. Papa noticed that Bucky had not reacted to his pronouncement. He had no fear in his eyes. This further angered the old ram.

"Leave the flock. Now."

Papa stamped his front hoof hard on the ground. But Bucky did not flinch.

Papa's blood boiled. He snorted and grunted and scratched the ground with his hoof.

"This is your final warning."

Papa grunted, lowered his head and took two steps back.

A fire was burning in Papa's eyes. The ewes held their breaths.

"You're asking for it, you insolent wether."

Papa leaped forward and charged. He sprung up on his hind legs and threw all his weight at Bucky with great force.

Bucky lunged forward.

The two rams butted heads with a crack.

Papa staggered back from the collision. He shook his head trying to regain his focus and composure.

Bucky stood in front of him watching him calmly.

Fury ignited in Papa's eyes. He charged again. Bucky raised up on his hind legs, threw his head back, then snapped it forward. Their heads smashed together with a hollow clunk.

Papa was stunned by the blow. He staggered backward. His eyes were unfocused and his legs wobbled. He dropped on his front knees causing the ewes to gasp again. Papa quickly regained his faculties and sprung up onto his feet.

"I'm warning you, Bucky. I'm not going to hold back my next charge. I don't want to kill or maim you but I can't make any guarantees. For your own sake, I order you to leave the flock or else."

"I'm not leaving, Papa."

"This will end badly for you, son."

Papa stepped back staring into Bucky's eyes. Papa's eyes narrowed. He inhaled deeply, steeled himself and charged. Bucky took three steps back and burst forward in a flash. He lifted up on his hind legs, pulled his head back and then jerked it forward with great speed and force.

The two rams clashed with a mighty crack. Papa's body went stiff. He was unconscious as he fell sideways in the mud with a thump. His eyes were open and rolled back in his head. He lay still in the grass with four legs extended stiffly from his torso.

Bucky walked up to him and sniffed him. The old ram's breathing was deep and erratic.

"Oh, Bucky," Lulu said. "Are you OK?"

The ewes gathered around him and looked at him in awe.

"Are you hurt, Bucky?"

"I hope you're not in pain."

"Let me tend to your wounds."

Bucky walked forward through the flock. The sheep parted in front of him and followed behind him as he walked through the grass. He walked out to where the grass was greenest. Lulu stayed close, nipping at ewes who pressed in toward Bucky.

He looked over at Papa who lay stiffly on his side. Not one ewe paid the slightest attention to the old ram lying unconscious on the ground.

Bucky felt pity for Papa and a certain contempt for the ewes—at how readily they had abandoned all concerns for Papa and transferred them to himself.

All their eyes were on him but he ignored them and began to graze. They followed his lead and grazed. They gravitated toward him while Lulu did her best to ensure they kept their distance.

Bucky noticed the shepherd and the dog on the hill had been watching the proceedings below.

Mama approached through the grass. Lulu stood between Bucky and his mother, but Mama snorted and pushed Lulu out of the way with a snap of her head.

Lulu backed off and let the old matriarch pass.

"You're the leader of the flock now," Mama said. "I knew sooner or later this day would come, but I didn't think it would come so soon."

She pressed her muzzle against him and ran her nose up his neck.

"I'm proud of you, Bucky. But please, don't hold hard feelings for Papa. The two of you never saw eye to eye, but your father had many good qualities."

"I have no hard feelings for Papa."

She smiled. "There's greatness in you, Bucky. I've always known it." She touched her nose to his. "My little Bucky."

Eventually, Papa came to. He sat on his knees watching over the grass all the ewes that had gathered around Bucky. It was late afternoon when Papa staggered up onto his feet. He stood alone in the grass away from the flock.

The shepherd whistled from up on the hill. Stevie ran down through the grass to the flock. He ran up to Bucky.

"The whistle was the signal. You know what to do, Bucky."

Bucky stood looking down at the dog.

"I don't want any trouble," Stevie said. "I know we've had our differences. But you're the leader of the flock now. Leaders gain privileges but also responsibilities. I'm here to help you, Bucky. We can work together."

Bucky looked down at the dog without moving.

"You know, you remind me of another ram I once knew. He was a great leader. I see him in your eyes. I think you can be a great leader of the flock like him. I want to help you do that. I think the two of us can make a great team."

"Please, Bucky," Mama said. "Don't let us down. Do what you're supposed to do."

The shepherd whistled again.

"What are you going to do, Bucky?" Stevie asked.

Papa trotted slowly up the hill to the shepherd. But none of the ewes followed. They all watched and waited for Bucky to make his next move.

Bucky turned and trotted up the hill to the shepherd.

"You and I or going to make a great team, Bucky," Stevie said.

Stevie ran to the back of the flock and nipped and harassed the stragglers.

The flock followed Bucky up the hill. They ran past Papa and then through the gate into the corral. Bucky was first to the trough. He ate from it as the sheep approached hesitatingly. He snorted and stomped a hoof and they backed off. He ate the freshest alfalfa before allowing the ewes to feed.

Papa stood against the fence away from the flock. He looked over at the trough but didn't approach it.

At dusk, Rancher Dave's truck pulled up alongside the corral. It slowed with a squeal of brakes. Pedro opened the corral gate and slammed it shut behind him. He walked up to Papa and slapped the old ram hard on the rump.

"Go, sheeple. Go into the chute."

The shepherd pushed and shoved Papa up the chute and into the trailer.

Papa looked out longingly into the corral from the trailer. He looked over at Bucky and then turned his eyes away.

Bucky walked across the corral up to the fence and looked at his father through the slats. Papa couldn't bring himself to look Bucky in the eyes.

"You've defeated me. Now I go to greener pastures."

"No, Papa. They're not taking you to greener pastures."

Truth

"I'm going to greener pastures."

"Listen to me, Papa. There are no greener pastures. I don't know where they're taking you, but if you see a chance, try to escape. Try to find your way back to the flock."

Papa's eyes were downcast. He couldn't bring himself to look Bucky in the eyes.

"The flock is yours now."

"Pay attention to the road and the hills so you can remember the way back. When the humans let down their guard, make a run for it. Try to come back to us. I'll protect you."

"Come back to the flock? I can't face the ewes like this. I've been defeated and humiliated."

"Then run to Liberty Mountain. Zeus is there with his wild flock."

"There's danger beyond the fence."

"There's danger. But there's freedom, too."

Papa shook his head. "I never thought this day would come. I thought the flock would always be mine—that all the ewes and all the best feed were my birthright. I came to believe it. I didn't see the potential in you—that you would take it all away from me."

"I'm sorry, Papa."

"It's all yours now—the ewes and the best feed and the respect and admiration. You're the important one now. I see your youth and strength. I'm old. My time is done here. It's time for me to go. I'm ready for greener pastures."

"Don't trust the humans, Papa. They don't have your best interests in mind. Listen to me. If you see the opportunity, make a run for it."

"You've already defeated me and humiliated me. Why do you try to put fear and doubt in my mind? I want to go to greener pastures."

"Papa, listen to me. There are no greener pastures."

"No. I believe there are."

The truck's engine rattled to life. The trailer pulled away from the corral. Bucky watched it disappear behind the oaks in the fading light.

He stood in the center of the flock in the dark. All the ewes were around him. Lulu stayed close pressing herself against him while fending off any other ewe who tried to do the same.

Soon they were all asleep. But Bucky remained awake for hours staring into the darkness.

He awoke in the morning chill. Mist drifted up from the mud in the dim light of dawn.

Pedro emerged from his camper and trudged over to the corral. He opened the gate.

"Let's go, Bucky," Stevie barked. "Get 'em moving."

Bucky trotted out the gate and down the hillside through the frosty grass. The flock followed behind him.

He fell easily into his new role, quickly realizing the benefits of being the leader of the flock. He enjoyed the attention and affection of the ewes. He enjoyed seeing the pride in his Mama's eyes when she looked upon him. The shepherd watched over them and the dog protected them. No coyotes harassed them. Life was good here. Life was easy.

The rains came and went and the days grew longer. Yellow mustard flowers, orange poppies, purple shooting stars and blue lupins blanketed the green hillsides with splashes of color. The leaves returned to the oaks and sycamores. The warm sunshine brought new energy to the flock. The excitement in the ewes at having a new, youthful and vigorous leader seemed electric.

Bucky and Mama often grazed together. They enjoyed each other's company. They chatted about this and that for hours on end—about the return of spring and the beauty of the flowers and the new leaves on the trees. About the ground squirrels and the rabbits and deer, the hawks and eagles and jays. They enjoyed telling each other about the observations they'd made of all they'd seen—the way the hawks ride the wind currents in the sky above, the way the sun crosses the sky each day to warm the earth and how the stars and the moon light up the dark night. Mama was the only sheep in the flock he could talk to about such things. The other sheep didn't seem to notice much about their surroundings unless it had to do with food or some potential danger they felt might harm them. When

Bucky talked to the ewes, they would listen and nod their heads with infatuated but uncomprehending eyes. There was no point talking to them.

Bucky looked up at the shepherd sitting on a rock reading a book on the hillside.

"I don't understand you, Mama. You observe the world around you and think things through. But you refuse to think about the humans. Why don't you ever talk about them?"

"The shepherd watches over us, Bucky."

"I know you don't like to hear it, but the only reason he watches over us is because one day the humans will come in their trucks and take us away and eat us. The shepherd watches over us and the dog protects so that other predators don't eat us before they do. The humans are the most dangerous predators of all, above all others. Sooner or later, they'll come for us and take us away like they did to Papa."

"The shepherd watches over us. That's enough for us to know."

"I don't understand why you can't see the truth."

"I see a happy flock that is safe from harm with plenty of food to eat."

"The humans keep us here because they're want to kill us and eat us."

Mama looked up from the grass and gazed upon him as she chewed her cud.

"Why can't you accept the truth? You even saw it with your own eyes in the slaughterhouse."

"I was a lamb when Zeus told us that the humans were going to eat us. After he left, I often thought about what he'd said. I couldn't believe it.

But I watched the humans and their ways. I eventually understood that Zeus was right."

"You've known the truth all this time? And you kept it from me. You lied to me."

"Bucky, you got your smarts from me. We see things the other sheep can't. We understand things. But sometimes it's better not to understand. We lead a good life here. A happy life. I know that someday the humans will come and take me away. But what am I supposed to do? Run away into the wilderness? To be chased by coyotes and mountain lions and feral pigs? For what? To live on the side of a mountain in constant fear of being torn apart by predators, not knowing if I will have forage to eat the next day? Think things all the way through, Bucky."

"There's freedom outside the fence, Mama."

"Freedom from what? Freedom from want? From fear? From all the dangers and hardships of the wild?"

"The sheep on Liberty Mountain are free. Greg and I saw it with our own eyes."

"And where is Greg now?"

Bucky fell silent. He looked at Mama blankly for a moment, then looked down sullenly at the grass.

"Bucky, we're sheep. Sooner or later we all get eaten. I understand that, but I'd rather live here in safety than in uncertainty and fear. The shepherd watches over us and the dog protects us. I'm happy knowing that. I'm happy here with the flock."

"How can you be happy knowing the truth?"

"I put it out of my mind. Instead, I pay attention to the beauty of the world—to the hills and the flowers and the trees and deer. I enjoy the company of my friends and my family. I'm happy here being with you."

"I can't put it out of my mind, Mama."

"We have a good life here. An easy life. It fills my heart with pride seeing you all grown up and taking your place at the head of the flock. You're the leader now. It's what I've always wanted for you. Let's not talk about the humans any longer. Let's put them out of our minds and pretend they don't exist. Please, Bucky. Will you do that for me? For your Mama who loves you?"

The days came and went passing uneventfully. Every morning, Bucky led the flock from the corral out onto the hills. Every evening, they returned to the corral. The nights were cool but the chill had lost its bite. Bucky stayed awake in the corral as the flock slept. He stayed awake in the darkness thinking until finally slipping into sleep.

Bucky grazed in the green grass with the flock on a sunny afternoon, waiting for the shepherd's call. The evening approached. The sun was setting behind the coastal mountains, painting the sky in fiery orange and red. The colors were fantastic, more brilliant than he ever remembered. Purple and pink and green and scarlet illuminated the sky in vivid and shifting color.

As Bucky gazed upon the roiling sky, he spotted Greg grazing alone across the field. Bucky left the flock and walked through the grass to him. Greg looked up and watched Bucky approach.

"It's good to see you, Greg."

The old sheep looked healthy and content. He belched. Then smiled his gap-toothed smile.

"I'm sorry for the mean things I said to you."

"Hmph."

Greg lowered his head and grazed on the grass. The two sheep grazed together beneath the burning sky.

The shepherd whistled. The dog barked and ran down the hillside.

"I have to go," Bucky said.

Greg looked up at him. He winked and turned and looked toward Liberty Mountain. He looked back at Bucky. "You're one crazy sheep."

The old ram walked through the grass to the mountain that was silhouetted against the spectacular colors of the sun that was setting behind the jagged peak.

Bucky awoke in the morning chill with the vision vivid in his mind's eye. Pedro opened the gate.

"Let's go, Bucky," Stevie barked. "Get 'em moving."

Thinking Things Through

The flock grazed under the oaks on a beautiful spring day without a cloud in the sky. The sky was a clear and dazzling blue. A light breeze drifted through the oak branches that were now covered with waxy green leaves. Sunlight filtered through the leaves that fluttered in the wind. Yellow mustard flowers blanketed the grass between the trees. Blossoms were everywhere, dashing the green hills with vibrant color.

Lulu stayed close always keeping an eye on Bucky. He stopped grazing and watched her as he chewed his cud. They had grown up together and had always been close. She had played king of the hill with him and Billy and Tom and Ricky. They had been so happy then exploring the pasture and frolicking in the grass without a care in the world.

Lulu was no longer a lamb but an adult ewe, young and healthy, plump and well formed. She was far and away his favorite ewe in all the flock.

Lulu noticed that he was looking at her. She batted her eyelashes and looked away bashfully.

Bucky beckoned her with a nod of his nose. She smiled and walked up to him through the grass and yellow flowers.

"Yes, Bucky?"

"Look over there."

He nodded with his nose to a clearing between the trees where a skunk was rooting in the dirt.

Lulu stiffened at the sight of it. "Oh, my goodness. What is it?"

Her inclination was to run. But Bucky stayed put so she did as well. The black and white creature had a long striped tail that stuck up into the air as it dug through the dirt with its front claws.

"Is it dangerous?"

"Very dangerous."

"Bucky, I'm scared. Let's run away."

"It's only dangerous if you frighten it."

"Does it eat sheep?"

Bucky laughed. "It's a little small to eat a sheep, don't you think?"

"It is quite small. What's so dangerous about it?"

"When it's frightened it turns around, lifts its tail and sprays you with a foul liquid. It's the stinkiest thing you've ever smelled. The stink sticks to you for weeks."

"So it makes you stink?"

"That's its defense. It makes you stink so bad you'll never want to mess with it again."

"Well, I don't want to stink. Let's go."

Four black and white kits emerged from their den at the base of an oak. The little kits ran to their mother.

"It's a mama skunk," Bucky said. "Those are her babies. Aren't they something?"

"Please, Bucky. I'm frightened. Let's go."

"Let's go talk to them."

Bucky stepped forward through the grass. But Lulu stepped back, snapping a fallen branch with a loud crack.

The skunks scurried away and disappeared down their burrow.

"Thank goodness they're gone."

"You scared them. Good thing she didn't spray us."

"Let's go, Bucky. I don't want to stink."

Bucky returned to grazing beneath the trees. Lulu stayed with him, nervous about the skunk. But soon the skunk was forgotten and she grazed next to him peacefully.

Lulu wasn't the greatest conversationalist, but Bucky enjoyed her company. He knew she adored him and he enjoyed her affection.

They moved along the hillside grazing through the grass until the morning turned to afternoon. The sun was warm and pleasant through the trees.

Bucky recognized this hill. He saw the barbed wire fence down below and the cows in the pasture beyond the fence.

"Follow me, Lulu."

Bucky walked down the hill and across the field away from the flock. Lulu followed beside him. She kept looking over her shoulder back up the hill toward the flock.

"Bucky, the flock must stay together."

"That's what sheep say."

"Where are we going?"

"Let's sneak away. Just the two of us. Walk with me."

"Oh, Bucky. You're so romantic."

The sheep grazed up on the hillside not noticing that their leader was walking away from them. Bucky and Lulu came to a rocky outcropping. Atop the outcropping was a gnarled and twisted oak that reached upward into the cloudless sky. The oak branches were covered with waxy leaves that were a newly fresh green. Orange poppies grew around its base and between the boulders. Steller's jays with blue feathers and crests atop their heads were up in the branches calling to each other and hopping from branch to branch.

Bucky walked between the boulders and around the oak. He emerged on the other side of the outcropping where the ground sloped upward toward the barbed wire fence.

He stopped at the bottom of the incline.

"Let's go back, Bucky. Stevie's going to notice we're gone. He'll be mad if he finds us here."

"You know, Lulu. If a sheep were to run up this slope and then leap from the top, he could jump right over the fence."

"Why would any sheep want to do that?"

"To get to the other side."

"But there's danger on the other side of the fence."

"There's danger. But there's freedom, too."

"Oh, Bucky. You say the strangest things sometimes. Let's go back. I bet the whole flock has noticed we're gone by now. They're going to be worried sick when they don't see us."

"If I jump over the fence, will you follow me?"

"Bucky, you're frightening me."

"We're both young and strong. We could move quickly through the hills and up the foothills to Liberty Mountain. Zeus is up there with his wild flock. We can join them. It's like heaven up there."

"Bucky, you're the leader of the flock. Please don't talk this way. It scares everyone."

"Follow me, Lulu. Follow me if you want to be free."

Bucky took two steps back, raised up on his hind legs, then galloped up the slope. He leaped from the top and soared over the fence. He landed on the other side with a clop of his hooves and skidded to a stop.

"Bucky!"

Bucky turned and looked at her through the barbed wire.

"Bucky, come back! There's danger beyond the fence!"

Bucky turned and trotted up the gravel road along the fence past the rows of the vineyard.

King of the Mountain

The ewes birthed their lambs late in the spring. Pedro helped with the more difficult births, pulling the lambs by their legs from their mothers' wombs.

The ewes licked their newborns and tended to them in the grass. The little lambs struggled up to their feet on wobbly legs and nursed from their mothers who cared for their newborns with gentleness and maternal affection.

The sheep of the flock had been rudderless without a leader. They'd been sullen and frightened when they'd learned that Bucky had left them. The few rams in the flock strutted around and jostled for dominance, but none was comparable to Bucky or Papa. In the absence of a dominant ram, Mama stepped forward to lead the flock. At first she had been reluctant, but she was the biggest of the older ewes, and the role fell naturally to her. The other ewes were occupied by their newborns while Mama was without a lamb this year. She had been with the flock long enough and knew what to do. When the shepherd opened the corral in the mornings, she trotted out first through the gate down the hillside and the ewes and their lambs followed behind her. When the shepherd whistled in the evenings, she ran up the hill and back to the corral and the flock followed. She did her best to keep the ewes and the playful lambs from wandering off. She watched over the lambs and did her best to help the ewes keep them out of trouble. She and Stevie worked well together and quickly came to an understanding. They worked in tandem and kept the flock together.

But for the most part, Mama kept to herself. She didn't chitchat with the ewes or dawdle through the grass with them like she used to do. They didn't gravitate to her like they did to the rams, but they appreciated her maternal instincts, respected her as their matriarch, and followed her without question. The sheep needed a leader to follow and Mama filled the role as well or better than any ram could.

The weather grew warmer and the rains ceased. On some afternoons, the air became hot, giving them a taste of the summer heat to come.

The blossoms faded and slowly the hills turned from green to brown. The nights were cool and pleasant but by noon each day the heat radiated in waves from the drying grass.

Rattlesnakes returned with the heat, emerging from their hiding places to sun themselves on exposed rocks. They rattled their tails whenever a sheep wandered near.

Early one morning, a team of men arrived. They sheared the sheep in the back of a trailer and castrated the male lambs. The poor males bleated and cried in pain, returning to their mothers with timid and fearful looks in their eyes.

But the pain soon receded and the lambs were again playing in the fields and on the hillsides. Every boulder, tree stump and pile of dirt was fought over in energetic contests of king of the hill.

Mama took little pleasure in watching the lambs at play. A darkness had settled over her. When she grazed, her dark mood weighed heavily on her. She missed Bucky terribly and was hurt that he had abandoned the flock. She was hurt that he had abandoned her. She wished there was something she could have done or said that would have made him stay. But in her heart, she knew he was too headstrong. He always had a mind of his own.

By late summer, the hills were dry as dust. The temperature soared. The sun blazed down relentlessly on the parched hills. The wind whipped up dust that gusted through the arroyos and across the hillsides. The once lush fields seemed stark and lifeless in the harsh midday heat.

But when the sun dipped low on the horizon, the sunlight softened and the hills became golden in the fading afternoon light. Mama liked to stand on the hilltops in the golden light and look out at the landscape and at Liberty Mountain in the distance. She imagined Bucky there atop the distant peak with Zeus and his wild flock.

One hot morning, the workers returned in their trucks and pushed the young males through the chute and into the trailers. The ewes baaed and bleated as the trucks pulled away from the corral. The lambs were taken away to greener pastures, so they told themselves.

Late in the summer the wildfires returned. Grass fires sparked in the foothills and mountains and raced through the dry grass and brush. Massive columns of smoke rose like pillars into the atmosphere and spread outward with the wind currents. The sheep could smell the smoke and soot in the air, but the wildfires were far off in the distance and never a threat to their corner of the hills.

Toward the end of summer, large tarantulas emerged from their burrows. The black spiders, as big as a human hand, crawled everywhere across the land—through the grass and over boulders and up tree trunks. The male tarantulas were on the move in search of mates.

Mama wished Bucky were here to observe and discuss this annual phenomenon. Every time she spotted some creature that lived here in the hills—a rabbit or a squirrel or a crow—she thought of Bucky. She missed him and worried about him. She worried about coyotes, wild pigs and mountain lions. She worried and feared that predators might have taken him. She worried about the danger beyond the fence. She worried that stray sheep get eaten.

She wished for a message or a sign that would somehow let her know he hadn't been eaten and was alive and healthy and well. But the months passed and no sign came.

Fall came suddenly. One day it was hot and the next a chill was in the air. The days shortened and the nights grew colder. The rains returned. But this year wasn't nearly as wet as last. Slowly, the brown hills turned green again.

One late afternoon, the flock grazed in a field as the sun dipped low on the horizon. Pedro sat on a rock smoking a cigarette and reading a book. Stevie lay in the grass by his feet.

Mama grazed with the flock. In front of her a monarch butterfly landed on a thistle. She watched the beautiful creature slowly open and close its orange-speckled wings. She thought of Bucky as she gazed on the butterfly. She could almost hear his baas carrying to her on the wind.

She heard his baa in the distance and thought her mind was playing tricks on her. She heard it again and raised her head and searched the grass and the hills with her eyes and swiveling ears.

On a hilltop atop a rocky outcropping stood a mighty ram with curling, spiral horns. Mama baaed. The big ram baaed back.

She would know that baa anywhere.

She baaed again. All the sheep of the flock raised their heads from the grass and looked up to the hilltop.

The shepherd stood up from his rock and shaded his eyes from the sun as he looked up at the ram atop the hill. Stevie jumped to his feet.

Bucky stood on the rocks with the evening sky behind him. He was fully grown, huge, muscular and magnificent. Bucky's mighty form was outlined against the golden sky.

Maria climbed up from behind the hillside and stood on the rocks beside him. A lamb climbed up on the rocks and stood with them.

All the sheep of the flock looked up at the ram, the ewe and the lamb atop the hill. Mama baaed and bleated.

Bucky nodded his head.

"My little Bucky."

The sheep of the flock all baaed. Stevie barked.

Mama looked over her shoulder with worry that Stevie would chase Bucky and his family away. But the dog remained at the shepherd's side, both looking up at the mighty ram on the hill.

Mama looked back up to the hilltop. But Bucky was gone, never to be seen again.

THE END

Gus Flory is the author of GALAXY OF HEROES
and THE PSYCHIC.